The Lost Days

Rob Reger *and* Jessica Gruner

The Lost Days

Illustrated by

Rob Reger *and* Buzz Parker

HARPER

An Imprint of HarperCollinsPublishers

www.harperteen.com

Library of Congress Cataloging-in-Publication Data

Reger, Rob.
Emily the Strange : the lost days / by Rob Reger and Jessica Gruner ; illustrated by Rob Reger and Buzz Parker. — 1st ed.
    p.   cm.
"HarperTeen."
Summary: Emily the Strange has lost her memory and finds herself in the town of Blackrock with nothing more than her diary, her slingshot, and the clothes on her back.
ISBN 978-0-06-145229-1 (trade bdg.) — ISBN 978-0-06-145230-7 (lib. bdg.)
[1. Amnesia—Fiction. 2. Identity—Fiction. 3. Goth culture (Subculture)—Fiction. 4. Runaways—Fiction. 5. Adventure and adventurers—Fiction.]
I. Gruner, Jessica. II. Parker, Buzz, ill. III. Title.

PZ7.R2587El 2009   2008027225
   [Fic]—dc22   CIP
                                                                 AC

Typography by Amy Ryan
09 10 11 12 13 SCP 10 9 8 7 6 5 4 3 2 1
❖
First Edition

For the world of Emily fans,
who get lost while never losing their ways

OK.

I think I better take some notes, cuz something super strange is happening to me, and I don't know

1. my name
2. anyone else's name
3. where I am
4. how I got here
5. where I live
6. how old I am (am I a kid or just short?)
7. anything I've done since I was born
8. whether I'm a cat person or a dog person
9. whether I actually believe people are either cat people or dog people
10. what might have been written on the eleven pages that were torn out of this notebook
11. why this happened to me
12. how long it's going to last, or
13. what I should do next.

Here's what I DO know:

1. I'm human.
2. I'm a girl.
3. I'm wearing a black dress.
4. I'm wearing black stockings.
5. I have long black hair.
6. I seem to like the color black.
7. I recently stepped in gum.
8. My skin is pale, so the bruises on my left arm show up really well.
9. I have a notebook, a pencil, and a slingshot, and that's it.
10. I'm left-handed.
11. I speak English.
12. The Earth is round and travels around the sun.
13. I seem to like the number 13.

Later

I'm in a town called Blackrock, according to the newspaper. I'm not sure whether a town this small even needs a newspaper. Too bad I can't remember any other towns to compare it to. Here's what I've seen: two streets, maybe fifteen buildings, and then dust plains all around. Almost everything—natural and human-made— is some shade of beige. There's a bus depot. A couple of stores. One tiny patch of grass that's passing for a park.

It seems quiet and peaceful here, but for some reason I prefer to assume it's crawling with menace and secret abominations.

Not sure if that says more about Blackrock or about ME.

Anyway. New things I know:

1. Nothing here looks familiar.
2. Nobody in Blackrock seems to know me.
3. Many people in Blackrock think I'm worth staring at.
4. Strange dogs don't always like to be petted.
5. I'm not a dog person.
6. There is never an Amnesia Recovery Center around when you need it.
7. Someone might be worried about me, but that someone is nowhere to be found.

What I can see of myself.

8. I will probably be sleeping on the streets tonight.
9. I'm hungry.
10. Food costs money.
11. I don't have any money.
12. Amnesia sucks rocks: big . . . black . . . rocks.
13. You can get a ticket in Blackrock for using a slingshot to entertain passersby.

At least I know what I look like now.

Later

Got fed. Here's how it went down: When the police told me to get out of their sight, I ducked into this café called the El Dungeon. Even though it was el dubious. El dungheap. Asked the chick behind the counter if she happened to have any free food. She said I could sweep the floor. Honk! I needed a shovel! Well, at least in the corners, where people had kicked most of the larger garbage.

Even taking my total amnesia into account, I think it's a pretty safe bet to say this is the ugliest building I've ever seen. Inside: Peeling paint on some walls, embarrassing wood paneling on others; splintery old furniture; and these dinged-up windows that rattle whenever a car goes past. There's a rickety staircase that apparently goes upstairs to Filthy Cobweb Land. And the music doesn't exactly brighten up the ambience—some kind of haunted whispering from the radio that sounds like a ghost town from 100 years ago, harmonizing with the espresso machine giving its death rattle.

So it's not the cheeriest place, or even the cleanest. But actually . . . it suits me just fine. Interesting.

Outside: The El Dungeon's worst feature is its unfortunate, and very thick, all-over coat of beige paint. Second-worst feature would have to be the large . . . SHAPES . . . on the roof. No telling what they are. Oversized beige sculptures of chewed gum or something. Other than that, hard to say WHAT the building looks like, since the paint is so thick it's hiding what might have been architectural details.

I was carrying something like the twenty-third dustpan of kipple to the Dumpster out back when I decided for sure that unless, or until, I could reverse my amnesia with a strategic head bump, I was going to set up camp in the alley behind the El Dungeon. El Dreamland! Multiple fascinating well-stocked Dumpsters! Enough building materials for a lovely lean-to! Animal friends! I made buddy-buddy with the local cats using savory treats found in garbage. Am hoping they repay the favor tonight, especially if it's nippy. Nothing like a seventeen-cat fur coat when it's nippy.

Am now sitting at a table in the café, eating a sandwich and checking out the customers. All seven of them. They look normal enough, aside from not moving the whole time I've been here. Anyway, at least I'm not getting stared at quite as much as I was outside. Hope I can tolerate hanging out here for a while.

Later

Talked with CounterChick, whose name is Raven.

COUNTERCHICK:	Hey, kid.
ME:	[Oh. She means me. Guess I AM a kid, and not just short.] . . . Yeah?
CC:	Uhhhhhhhhh. 'Nother sandwich?
ME:	Yeah, thanks. [Long period of silent eating.]
CC:	Yeah so.

ME: Yeah.

CC: Name's Raven. What's yours?

ME: Earwig. [Don't even know why I said that. Could be all the earwigs I had to sweep up off that floor earlier. Or possibly the way Raven's ears stuck out funny from under her wig. Pretty sure it's not my actual name.]

R: Uhhhhhhhhhh huh.

ME: Yeah.

It went on for a while like this. After a few minutes of not-too-scintillating chitchat, I could see she was mustering up to some kind of pointed question, which ended up going just a little bit like this:

Raven.

R: Yeah, so, Earwig.

ME: Yeah.

R: Uhhhhhhhhhhh, you live around here?

[I'd been dreading this question. Luckily I'd had lots of time while shoveling the floor to ponder a perfect response.]

ME: Nah.

R: Uhhhhhhhhhhh, that's cool.

ORDER HERE

Then she got all embarrassed and quickly turned to the espresso machine and started making shot after shot that nobody had even ordered. It was kind of a sad display, especially because the machine was rattling and wheezing so badly, when I could tell it just needed a shim and a spot of solder. So I ducked out to the alley, found what I needed in the Dumpster, and came back to take care of business.

Here's some new stuff I know: You can do wonders for an ailing espresso machine with a hairpin and some gum. Patrons of the El Dungeon consider me a mechanical genius. Sometimes it's better to let a few shots of espresso go to waste than to drink nine all by yourself. A refrigerator box makes a very good lean-to.

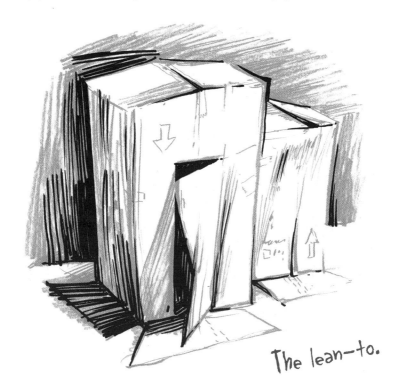

The lean-to.

Oh, and here's what my bruises look like.

Next Day

Again with the amnesia. This is getting old.

Later

Stared at myself in the mirror in the bathroom of the El Dungeon for a while, hoping it would bring something back. No luck.

Later

Roamed the streets of Blackrock, looking for clues about why I'm here. Nothing seems familiar. No LOST posters with my face on them, no urgent search parties. Just dirty looks. Makes me wonder if I caused some disgrace to this town before losing my memory.

I retraced my steps to the first spot I remember. Yesterday, when I came to, I found myself sitting on a park bench—you know, one of those pointless park benches with a plaque that commemorates someone who once did something and is now dead, in one of those tiny, pointless miniparks you see in small towns where the idea is to put a few square feet of grass and trees around a commemorative bench and pretend it's a park, so that the family of the dead important person isn't too offended. This one was about a block from the El Dungeon and had a completely pointless ten-foot wrought-iron gate (with no fence to go with it), a tiny patch of grass, and a tree. And the bench was commemorating an Emma LeStrande, Founder of Blackrock and Owner of its First Hotel and Café. Oh boy. Small town indeed!

Anyway, I went there and sat on the bench to think about what happened. I thought back to that moment—coming out of a muddled kind of daydream and realizing I didn't have a clue where I was, or WHO I was. Looking down, seeing the notebook in my hands, flipping through it searching for clues. Not even a name written inside. Feeling like I needed to document everything in case there are clues that I'm not able to recognize yet. Feeling the slingshot in my pocket. A slingshot?? I mean—random! Not knowing ANYTHING. I mean, I knew the sky is blue and cats don't fly—but I didn't (DON'T) know the first thing about myself.

As I sat there remembering yesterday, I started to sort of space out just staring at my arms and my hands, which might as well

The park—first thing I remember.

have belonged to someone else. The tiny scars. The little hairs. All those details must have been so familiar to me just a day ago and are now so completely foreign.

Sat there feeling depressed and frightened and sorry for myself for a while, then cheered up by thinking maybe my life had been really terrible and worth forgetting.

Anyway. Did some detective work around the minipark. The only semi-interesting items were under the bench: a candy wrapper, a couple of bottle caps, some ABC gum, a lot of round rocks that would be very nice for slingshotting, a pencil stub full of bite marks, 7 cigarette butts, a soda can, 27 cents in change, and yesterday's newspaper. From which I have learned that they really need to clean up their public ~~parks~~ park in this town. Litterbugs.

I pocketed the change (OK, yes, and some of the rocks, and also the newspaper) and headed back to the El Dungeon for lunch.

Later

Still hanging out at the El Dump. I mean, where else am I supposed to go? At least here no one stares.

Swept the floor, sorted junk mail, ate sandwiches, fixed broken cash register, eavesdropped on not-too-scintillating conversations, rescued six spiders from being stepped on, and found them homes in the corners of my lean-to. Told the local cats not to eat them. Found a broken Polaroid camera in the Dumpster. It looks newish, full of film, even. Fixed it within minutes. I am pretty sure this is not something most young people can do. I guess I know SOMETHING interesting about myself.

Hung out in the café for a while using up my film and making customers nervous. Meanwhile, people were coming in off the street for coffee to go, and Raven kept getting asked where Rachel was. She kept answering things like "Gone away." "Not here." "Iono." I guess Rachel used to work here. And Raven's apparently the brand-new girl, since everyone was asking her name. Man, the owner must have been desperate—I mean, she makes some pretty delicious espresso, but she can barely talk.

One of these friends of Rachel's asked who I was, and Raven said I was her assistant. The girl was all, "What are you, thirteen? Why aren't you in school?"

"Oh, I'm IN school," I told her, and Raven blushed and went to steam a bunch of milk no one had ordered. Hey, at least now I know how old I might be.

Later

Have read the Blackrock newspaper (all sixteen pages of it). From which I have learned that a town this small really DOESN'T need to have a newspaper.

Was also surprised to learn that a town this small has a museum. The Old Museum, to be exact. Will check it out later if I am in need of entertainment.

Later

Quite an exciting evening it turned out to be at the El Dungeon thanks to this fancy-pants named Ümlaut. He was nothing but trouble for Raven. At first I thought they had crushes on each other, but it turns out they are terrible enemies. But I don't think Ümlaut knows that.

He walked in around midnight. He was the most carefully dressed person in the El Dungeon, by a long shot. Lots of styling product in the hair. His accessories and grooming spoke of hours spent getting ready. Same with his eleven friends who piled in behind him. They were loud and had terrible vocabularies. It was all like:

"Snakebite, I pinked."

"Gor. We shoulda never grammed like that."

"What you get from a iceblink, huh."

and so on. After pestering Raven for quite a while with their espresso orders, they sat at the biggest table and totally dominated the place with some complicated card play, cackling laughs, and backdrafts of cologne. And then some of them started having this sort of dance contest, which mostly took place on top of the table; and some of them kind of ended up under the table, kicking the furniture with their fancy boots and making a ruckus about hamhocks and ravens, which clearly wasn't too welcomed by Raven. She was all hunched up under her cape, pretending to ignore them and looking blue.

Turn the page for a peek at the El Dungeon. ⟶

$3.25

either.

E.

$3.75

brew!

Ca

$4.75

milk.

Ma

$4.75

!

$4.75

emon.

$3.25

arm milk.

$4.00

extra rush.

$4.95

espresso.

Served with fr

The Reuben
Toasted and
sauerkraut.

Monte Cris
Ham, turk
Have it fri

Veggie S
Deliciou

.95

After a few more espressos they got rowdy and threw a bunch of furniture, broke some windows, did some violence to one another, and handed out stacks of cash to the police and to Raven. Then they all settled down again for another game of Calamity Poker.

I had been spying on them from behind the counter through a knothole that I had sort of helped along with a drill I found yesterday, all lonely and forlorn in the alley. It made a top-notch spyhole. I was all kind of hunkered down under the counter near Raven's knees. I'd been shooting coffee beans through the spyhole at the Ümlaut pack for a while. (Note to self: Coffee beans make excellent small-caliber ammo.)

Turns out I'm pretty good with a slingshot, but winging fashionistas on the ears and cuff links had gotten boring, so I started to talk to Raven.

ME: Hey, Raven.
RAVEN: [Whispering out of the corner of her mouth, like maybe she didn't want the Ümlauts to notice she was talking to someone crouched under the counter.] Uhhhhhhhh.

My new spyhole.

28

ME: Why don't you kick those people out?

R: Uhhhhhhhhhhhhhhhhh. They're, you know?

GuH! That Raven. It would take forever to write down our conversation, so let me just say that eventually I got it out of her (mostly through charades, and a LOT of fact-checking from customers) that Ümlaut runs a traveling medicine show called Professor Ümlaut's Prophylactery and Revue, and his old friend Attikol (who is, I guess, the only one of the inner posse not here tonight) runs the gun and doll show that travels with them, and that's called Uncle Attikol's Deadly Dollhouse. They just rolled into town two days ago, but they've been coming to Blackrock every year for at least ten years. And right now they are camped just outside town in the dust plains, putting on their lurid shows and selling their dubious potions to the townspeople. Also, they're rich. Good stuff. Will have to go out there tomorrow.

ÜMLAUT

29

Day 3

Seems I'm not bad at cat talk. All the spiders are still alive. Am being slept on by cats whenever it's nippy. The four black ones in particular like me a lot, and have pretty much banned the other cats from the fridge box.

What a pack of characters they are! One is an old lady with a white star around her eye. I think she's the leader. One of the boys has a missing eye, one has extra toes and white stripes on his tail, and one has a bandaged ear. Who would have bothered to bandage up an alley cat?

I went and gave them names: McFreely, Wily, Nitzer, and Cabbage. Which they don't answer to.

Later

This town is insane! I just got a $37 ticket for Unauthorized Photography of Historical Landmark. Guhh!! I'd looked up the address of the Old Museum, more accurately the Former Museum, although it is also probably the Ancient Museum, as well as the Startlingly Ugly Museum. What do you know—it's upstairs from the El Dungeon. Man, this town is small.

Wily

Nitzer

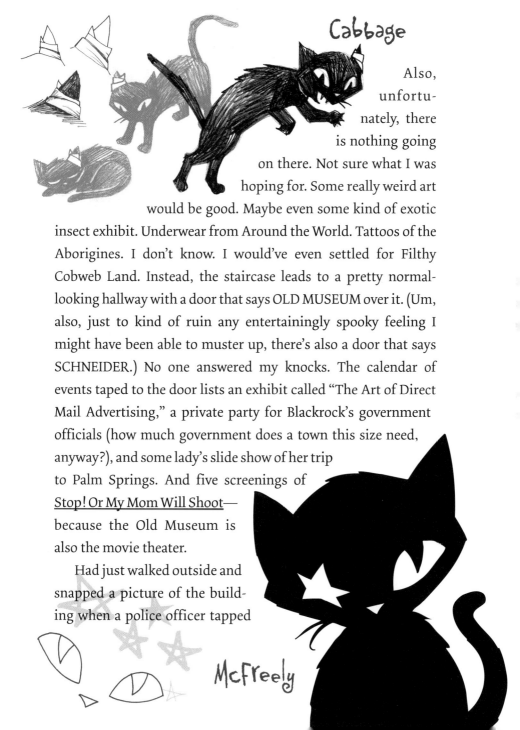

Cabbage

Also, unfortunately, there is nothing going on there. Not sure what I was hoping for. Some really weird art would be good. Maybe even some kind of exotic insect exhibit. Underwear from Around the World. Tattoos of the Aborigines. I don't know. I would've even settled for Filthy Cobweb Land. Instead, the staircase leads to a pretty normal-looking hallway with a door that says OLD MUSEUM over it. (Um, also, just to kind of ruin any entertainingly spooky feeling I might have been able to muster up, there's also a door that says SCHNEIDER.) No one answered my knocks. The calendar of events taped to the door lists an exhibit called "The Art of Direct Mail Advertising," a private party for Blackrock's government officials (how much government does a town this size need, anyway?), and some lady's slide show of her trip to Palm Springs. And five screenings of <u>Stop! Or My Mom Will Shoot</u>— because the Old Museum is also the movie theater.

Had just walked outside and snapped a picture of the building when a police officer tapped

McFreely

el Dungeon ¿ ?¿??

me on the shoulder and wrote me out the stupid $37 ticket. And then he didn't even ask me for the picture. So here it is.

UGH. Will continue my search for entertainment somewhere else.

Later

Have entertained myself somewhat by drawing a

little map of the town. I do mean little. Would never have bothered if it weren't such a pitifully little town. (Not sure it even deserved two pages, but I turned the next page to start anyway.)

Also, here's the town logo: ——>
I'm finding it very peculiar

CHARCOAL ALLEY

The town logo.

that the town is named Blackrock and even uses this silly logo of a tall mountainous black rock, a rock that has got to be imaginary, since the town seems to be in the middle of flatlands that just go on and on. No mountain or black rock in sight. I mean, Blackrock is actually sitting in a kind of dust bowl. Dust platter. Dust serving tray. Whatever. And not black dust, either, but beige and beiger, like all of the buildings.

And as if it needed to be any flatter here, that one tree at the minipark seems to be the only tree in Blackrock. Plenty of dead stumps, though. Seriously weird. Did the townspeople go on some kind of tree-killing, beige-painting spree, or what?

Later

Have just seen the shows of medicine, dolls, and guns. Mostly for lack of anything better to do. Was not expecting to find a major clue to my amnesia. Here's what happened. I was sitting in the back row of benches in the big tent where they were holding the demonstration of psychic powers. And this young kid, a little boy, was the psychic. I mean, of course I'm not saying he was actually psychic; those things are all a con. But anyway, he had the audience going. Bunch of rubes. He did some cheap parlor tricks like "Guess My Card" and "Where's My Snake?" And then his assistant, one of Ümlaut's fashionable crew, started walking around the audience so they could ask the kid questions about their love lives and "Am I gonna get sick?" and stuff.

I was just getting up to go when the assistant stuck the mic in my face. I didn't even say anything, just kept on going. And the next thing I knew, the kid was saying, "You can't remember a thing past two days ago, can you?"

Well, I got out of there quick. It was kind of scary. I haven't told ANYONE about having amnesia, so how else would he know, other than that . . . HE KNOWS?

Maybe he saw something happen to me.

Believe you me, I'm going to find out.

Am hiding out under the counter at the El Dungeon waiting to see if Ümlaut and his crew show up. Then I'll go look for the kid.

Jakey *mind reader* ·ツ·

Later

Have talked to the kid. I found him in his trailer playing video games. His name is Jakey and he goes by the Moon Child of the Valley of the Knowing. (!!!) He is nine years old and has been on the road all his life reading minds. He claims that he never saw me before today and that he is really psychic. I told him I didn't believe him but he told me the names I gave the cats earlier. Told him I wasn't convinced and he said that's cool, he had some high scores to beat, and could I close the trailer door softly so as not to disturb his parrot.

So much for that lead.

Really. Late. Can't. Sleep.

It just occurred to me that I don't know where Raven sleeps, or if she sleeps, because she's always behind the counter of the El Dungeon. Will investigate later and report back.

Even Later

Really couldn't sleep so I got out and roamed around Blackrock by night. I like it much better than Blackrock by day. Everything looks less beige by moonlight. Also very important: no people. Had those four black cats following me the whole way, except when I was following them, over fences and down alleys and such. They're not easy to see in the night. I guess neither am I.

I'm not sure, but at one point I thought the cats might be leading me somewhere on purpose. We had been walking around this kind of grim, antiseptic warehouse, just looking in windows and doing nothing in particular, and suddenly they all just darted under this fence, and I went after them and squeezed under, and they led me down this little service road, behind this other building to the left, and under this other fence, and while I was creeping under THAT fence, something got caught in my hair:

Then off we went running down this narrow walkway—and suddenly the cat in the lead, McFreely, the old lady with the starry eye, gave this killer hiss, and all the cats scattered just as the security officer stepped out in front of me. Even a few fake tears didn't get me out of that one, and I now owe the town $68 for After-hours Loitering.

Guess I need to learn that cat's warning hiss.

By the time I got back to the lean-to, it was so late it was early. Black cat posse was waiting for me, so I piled in with them nice and cozy. They all milled about for a bit, stepping on me and one another and muscling for their favorite spots (McFreely by my head; Cabbage on my feet; Wily and Nitzer in a complicated matrix across my stomach and arms), and of course it wasn't until everyone was finally settled that I remembered the cat collar still in my hair. Pulled it out and showed it to them. "Anyone here know Miles?" I asked. Well, what do you know? The half-blind guy, the

38

one I was calling Wily, stepped right up and meowed nice and clear. The collar fits him pretty well, too.

Day 4

Slept laaaaate and it was barely day anymore when I woke up. Had the most shattering nightmare. So devastating, I'm almost worried I may have severe psychological problems I just don't remember having.

The overall gist of this dream was that a giant lump of black candy, all molten and full of power, was buried under the El Dungeon. It sent up these invisible ineluctable sugar tentacles that tempted me to touch them. When I did, I got these huge sugar-shock rushes, so heavy they made my molars hurt. And I couldn't not touch the tentacles. And I knew that the lump of black candy was mine and I had to protect it. But all the time it was being attacked by underground creepy-crawly cave mutant people who licked and lapped at it, and there was nothing I could do. One by one the invisible sugar tentacles died, and the underground candy pool leaked away almost to nothing, and then suddenly I knew that when the last drop of candy was gone, my heart would stop beating, and I wouldn't be able to take a breath. And then my heart DID stop, and I woke up yelling "AIEEEE!" and all the cats jumped off me and went running down the alley.

Wow, my heart is thumping as I'm writing this down.

In fact.

It feels kind of good.

I think I LIKE nightmares.

Later

After my excellent nightmare I was feeling all productive. Went into the El Dungeon ready to take on the day (um, late afternoon, anyway). Swept the floor, performed basic maintenance on espresso maker and cash register, ate sandwiches, and tried to clean up Raven's back counter area a little. (I need more room to stretch my legs while spying.) A massive pile of junk mail had accumulated there since I sorted it all two days ago. I took pity on Raven, who if you ask me does not have the mental capacity for sorting junk mail, and went through it for her. After a long while sifting through ads, coupons, flyers, leaflets, and circulars, I was starting to notice that all of it looked suspiciously alike, and then I found something that explained it all: a glossy promotional postcard from Marshall Prepress & Printing, the local direct mail advertising company, who wished to offer the El Dungeon a special rate on its own glossy promotional postcard.

The only other item of interest was a flyer from the Blackrock Telecommunications Dept. encouraging everyone to be prepared for St. Clare's Day. A holiday of which I have no memory. Great. No telling what other holidays and basic knowledge of the world were lost in the amnesia.

Man, Raven owes me big. I think my soul died a little bit from reading that garbage.

Later, Much Later

Am sitting in the police station waiting for the police chief to see me. Am not happy. Here's what happened.

Had finished sorting the junk mail, dumped it all into a box, and walked it down to the post office. Stood in line for twenty minutes while some guy in front of me tried in vain to get his mail from the postmistress. He finally left, swearing to get his lawyer involved. I gave the postmistress the box of mail and told her we were tired of doing other people's recycling for them and would she please take our address off the junk-mail list.

POSTMISTRESS: Address.
[I gave it to her. She typed at her computer and stared at the screen, then at me.]
    PM: Your name.
    ME: Earwig.
    PM: [Glaring.] Your REAL name.
    ME: Uh, Raven.
    PM: Last name?
    ME: Uh, Dungeon.
    PM: Well, Miss Raven Dungeon, you are not listed as a resident at that address.
    ME: It's a business.
    PM: And you're not listed as the business owner.
    ME: So who is?
    PM: One moment.

She retreated into her back room. I was just leaning over the counter to get a look at her computer screen when the front door opened and a police officer came in.

POLICE OFFICER: Everything OK?

PM: [Rushing back into the room. Acting all huffylike.] Oh, Officer Summers, thank goodness you're here! This little . . . URCHIN . . . is, well, I don't know what she's trying to do, besides harass a tired postmistress half to death!

ME: [Silently heading for the door.]

PM: [Pointing at box of junk mail. Screeching.] You can't leave that here!

PO: [Standing in front of door. Blocking me from leaving.] What's your story, kid? Haven't seen you around. Name?

ME: Earwig . . . Raven . . . Dungeon . . .

PO: Your real name.

ME: I don't know.

PO: [Laughing. Having time of his life.] Oh boy! Chief is gonna love this! Let's move. Grab your box.

—Gotta go, the chief is ready to see me, more later.

Later

Spent about an hour at the police station saying "I don't know" over and over. Turning my pockets inside out to show them I had no ID. Telling them the story of my life as I knew it (i.e., the last four days). Good times, good times. "Put that slingshot away or I'll impound it." "Wipe that frown off your face or I'll GIVE you something to frown about." Farking bumwarks!

Was finally released when they got tired of hearing "I don't know" for the millionth time. Got off relatively easy, I think, with a $52 ticket for Impeding Postal Business. At first I thought it was really weird, not to mention really bad policework, that they did not check some kind of missing persons database for my picture. But then I thought about what the chief had said when he let me go: "Have your uncle come with you next time and we won't have to keep you so long." Which didn't make the least bit of sense until I thought of Uncle Attikol's Deadly Dollhouse. And how Ümlaut hands out stacks of cash to the police. And how the chief rubbed his fingers in that subtle "bribe me now" way when he said it.

So, they think I'm with the medicine show. Which makes me feel pretty sure I'm not from Blackrock. Also, it's not a bad alibi. Will introduce myself as Uncle Attikol's Amnesia Girl if I have any future police encounters.

Still, it was all very tiring, and I am now thinking seriously of ditching this weird town. Went down to the bus station and stared

at the destinations and arrivals schedule, hoping something would sound familiar and/or appealing. Nothing.

It's scary how, when I try to think past three days ago, the only thing I can remember is the feeling of how it is to remember. Not even the whisker of an actual memory. Do I live in a city? In a cave? In a tree house? Is it weird that I'm living in a lean-to made of a refrigerator box? Am I weird? The lady in the bus station stared at me like I was weird. Do I have parents? Friends? Pets? Do they miss me? Etc. Got myself so worked up into fake-missing people who might not even exist that I even cried a little fake tear, then got irked at myself for being a baby. No point getting sentimental until

I at least know what I'm missing. After all, I could be an orphan; or maybe my parents did this to me, maybe I'm better off without them.

Later

When I got over my fake-pity party, I picked up the cats at the lean-to, and then we went and roamed around the perimeter of town for a while enjoying the solitude. I kind of lost track of time, I guess. I sort of took a nap lying out there in the middle of the dust plain. When I woke up I could see all these stars. They were so great, and all I could think was, I bet I could see so many more if Blackrock would just turn out the lights for a bit.

Since I was already out on the edge of town, I decided to drop by ol' psychic Jakey's trailer and see if he was ready to cough up any interesting information about my amnesia. He was in the middle of a game.

> ME: Hey, Moon Child, what else do you know about my amnesia?
>
> JAKEY: I only know what you know. You don't know a lot.
>
> ME: Do you seriously believe you have psychic powers?
>
> J: Hey, wouldn't it have been nice earlier if Blackrock had just turned out the lights for a bit so you could see more stars?
>
> ME: . . . . OK.
>
> J: Also, just so you know, St. Clare's Day is some weird local holiday they have here. I mean, you didn't forget it or anything.
>
> ME: OK.
>
> J: Also, pretty much everyone in town works for the junk-mail company, so you might want to stop complaining about it unless you want everyone to hate you.
>
> ME: I said, OK.

What can I say? The kid has a talent. Still, he's useless to me.

Later

Fracketing bogcarts! Just when I was feeling better about my basic knowledge of the world, I suddenly discovered I do not remember the word for a baby cat. Am afraid to ask anyone. Am afraid to discover what other common words may have been lost in the amnesia. Am hoping I don't have any casual conversations that reveal I do not know the word for a baby cat. Probably safer to avoid all casual conversations, just in case.

Later

I found out that Raven has a little back room with a door that blends right into the awful wood paneling behind the counter. I spent the evening sitting as far away from her as possible, pretending to read the paper, while secretly spying. Also, keeping notes on the regulars and how long they stayed. I include a sample of my data for posterity. All names have been changed, or I guess made up, since I don't know anyone's actual name.

GRAPEY:	4 hours 7 minutes
SIZZLE AND PETAL:	3 hours 9 minutes
CURLS:	once for 5 hours and 15 minutes, again later for 3 hours and 20, then again for 4 hours and 45
HURK:	2 hours 17 minutes
STEVE:	between 2 and 3 hours
HAMHAWK:	11 hours 33 minutes

Back to Raven. While pretending to be extremely busy taking notes, or studying my shoe or something for clues to my identity, I was actually keeping a sharp half-eye on the counter region. All of a sudden she vanished. I mean, maybe I blinked for a microsecond longer than normal, but really, I was looking right at her, and she just vanished.

I glanced around really fast. Not a single customer was looking at the counter. She'd totally disappeared! With complete stealth I snuck to the counter, just in time to catch Raven slipping out through her homemade, wood-panel-camouflaged, no-doorknob-having, no-one-knows-I-went-to-the-breakroom secret little door. Pretty amazing, until I busted her using it. She didn't let on much, just made me a metric grip of sandwiches and much espresso.

Much! Espresso!! Later!!!

I've come up with a few possible scenarios of how I got here and lost my memory:

1. Something involving space travel and being from a planet other than Earth. Yes, I do SEEM human . . . Could I just be humanoid?
2. I was on a family trip when I . . . fell out of the car . . . and bumped my head . . . and my family is so large, or so absentminded, they still haven't noticed I'm missing.
3. I am a highly trained spy operating under cover so deep, my memories had to be erased.

4. I used to work with Rachel, previous employee of the El Dungeon, until Raven knocked us on the heads and took our jobs.

5. I used to work in Ümlaut's traveling medicine show until . . . yeah, see above.

6. I was living in a typical suburb of Anytown, USA, until I decided to escape my incredibly meaningless life by giving myself amnesia and hopping a bus to nowhere.

7. I was actually a cat named Earwig until being magically transformed into a human girl. By someone. For some reason.

8. I came here from 100 years in the future. The trip destroyed my memory.

9. I am a creature from another dimension.

10. I am a supernatural being recently risen from death.

11. I summoned myself out of the void.

12. I am a hologram.

13. I am the victim of a terrible practical joke.

All of these theories are flawed. Must find more clues.

Later

Took in some night air with the cats, and then later, walking back to my alley, who should I run into but (Very) Regular Customer Curls, on one of his short trips outside the El Dungeon. It better be said up front that Curls, first of all, thinks he is much more important and popular than he actually is. Also, even though he is probably only a couple years older than I am, he doesn't seem to spend much time at school, or at home for that matter, since he's putting in around twenty-seven hours a day at the El Dungeon. And he pesters Ümlaut's pack as much as they'll let him. Clear case of social climbing. You can tell by the complicated shirts, and how he's trying out conversational gambits on you all the time.

the extremely... hip... Curls! (Ugh.)

(VERY) REGULAR
CUSTOMER CURLS: Fancy meeting you here.
ME: Curls.
(V)RCC: Isn't it late for a missy without a sleeve to her name? What IS your name, anyway? Cockroach, right? No—Silverfish?
ME: Earwig.
(V)RCC: A ha haha ha! Sounds like a good nick- name for RAVEN, with those ears of

hers, and that wig . . . So, I heard you don't remember a thing past three days ago?

ME: [Turning and walking away.] Ugh. Later.

(V)RCC: Speaking of nicknames, Curls is a really stupid one. I prefer Ripper.

Day 5

Slept late and nearly missed the daylight completely. Huh, no big loss if you ask me. Unfortunately I did not sleep late enough to miss the chief of police, who came by to see if the Ümlaut posse had any heavy stacks of cash they needed taken off their hands. And like a good, efficient defender of the public peace, he took the opportunity to threaten me with a $123 ticket for unlicensed slingshot use.

I held out my innocent, empty hands. Raven gaped at us with her mouth open. Even Ümlaut and his crew halted their game of Calamity Poker to stare. "Slingshot?" I said. "I don't have a sling-shot."

The chief looked at Ümlaut, who just looked confused. "Errrrm . . . I don't see a slingshot, Chief," he finally managed to say. Then the two of them got into a long discussion of the town ordinances being violated today by the medicine show and how much it was going to cost.

I left them to it, and hid in the fridge box.

Later

A baby dog is a puppy. A baby kangaroo is a joey. A baby eel is an elver. A baby cat is a . . . lemon. A baby cat is a . . . pimple. A baby cat is a . . . mitten.

Am very frustrated.

Later

An adorable baby . . . pickle??

Questions:

1. How come the police are letting me camp out in a refrigerator box in the alley instead of offering me a place to stay indoors, or something?

2. Why is RAVEN just letting me camp out in a refrigerator box in the alley? And by the way, where and when does SHE sleep?

3. Does she look familiar or do I just want to think that?

4. Is she actually dull in the brain or do I just want to think that?

5. What DID happen to Rachel, former employee of the El Dungeon? Did she quit, was she fired, did she move away, did she just disappear? Or something . . . worse?

6. How'd I get those suspicious bruises on my arm?

7. How long does a medicine, gun, and doll show stick around a small town, usually?

8. Is their medicine as poisonous as it tastes?
9. How did Miles lose his collar, and where's his owner?
10. What if I still have amnesia a year from now? Or . . . 20 years from now?
11. Will I ever forgive my family for not coming to my rescue?
12. [Insert 1300 other questions I could ask about my family, myself, and my former life.]
13. Is it silly of me to think I'll figure this out by following "clues" when I haven't figured out a single thing in 5 days?

Later

Still no leads on my identity. Instead I am using my brainpower trying to figure out how Calamity Poker is played. After watching the Ümlaut crew play forty-odd games, I think I know the basic rules of gameplay. The person with the highest social rank (i.e., Ümlaut) is always the Dealer. The Dealer chooses everyone else's position at the table. The more the Dealer likes you, the closer you get to sit to him. The two players sitting the farthest from the Dealer (called the Beast and the Maiden) put money in the pot before the cards are dealt. Every player gets two cards face down. These are called the Ballroom Cards. Players who have recently offended the Dealer usually get their Ballroom Cards "accidentally" face up. In between rounds of betting, the Dealer puts three community cards (called the Knife, the Rope, and the

Candlestick) face up on the table.

Instead of being ranked, all hands have a point value, which usually has to be argued about for a long time at high volume before anything is decided. Cards can have different point values according to the day of the week, combination with other cards in the same hand, or phase of the moon. The Dealer makes the final decision on the value of each player's hand. If two (or more) players have hands of the same value, those players go into a Challenge

Calamity Poker in progress!

Round—usually a choice between Games of Chance; Embarrassing Truth; or Feats of Strength, Skill, and Endurance. And all Challenge Rounds are overseen and judged by the Dealer.

I've also noticed that bets under $500 are rare, and always laughed at. Man, how much money is that medicine show bringing in?

I should probably admit that the Ümlaut crew is turning out to be more entertaining than annoying, and I guess I could be wrong about Ümlaut being Raven's enemy. Maybe he's just more interesting that way. Seems like, in all the books and movies, whenever you have a rundown (but lovable) café frequented by a bunch of pathetic (but lovable) underdogs, then obviously the rich, obnoxious, fashionable out-of-towners who spend all their spare time there, drinking coffee and breaking furniture and, I don't know, secretly planning to buy it, bulldoze it, and turn it into a strip mall, have to be the enemy. Except in this case, I don't know if the café or the underdogs who come here are lovable. Or if there's really any problem with the Ümlauts spending their money breaking and replacing the El Dungeon's furniture. It's definitely not my concern why Raven tolerates them hanging out here. Actually, I think Raven, being Raven, would tolerate a lot of things even worse than Ümlaut. I could picture her, for example, putting up with a colony of plague rats nesting in her wig, without much of a fuss.

Also: I think it's peculiar that I seem to know something about "all the books and movies" when I can't actually remember any specific books or movies. And another thing: I keep getting this feeling that there's a song that really relates to my situation—being a stranger, even to myself, and thinking everyone around me is strange—but I don't remember a single actual song I may ever have known. Not even the one you sing to someone whose birthday it is.

Clearly my mind is very odd!!!

Later

More intrigue at the El Dungeon! Ümlaut's friend Attikol finally came in. You know, the guy who runs the Deadly Dollhouse. But instead of hanging out playing Calamity Poker like the other nuisances, all he did was flirt with Raven! I may have forgotten to mention that Raven is fairly gorgeous, and Attikol seemed kind of smitten. You wouldn't believe the lines he was spitting. I was embarrassed.

As usual, I was hiding under the counter, so I heard every word.

ATTIKOL: So, you're the new girl. My friend Ümlaut neglected to tell me you were such a dream incarnate.

RAVEN: Uhhhhhhhhhhh . . .

A: Ha. Ha. Ha. Oh, dear. Though the brightest light in the heavens may shine for man, it doth not shine for you. In your eyes, but never in your mind.

R: . . . . Thank you?

A: Did Ümlaut mention to you that I have magical powers beyond your wildest dreams?

Attikol

R: Uhh . . . no.

A: Right, well, I was just kidding. Seriously, though, I do have a great set of guns.

ME: [Snorting from under the counter.]

A: I look into your eyes, Raven, and what do I find? Nothing more than lint and espresso recipes. And this, my deadly doll, this is what drives me wild for you! I must have you!

R: Uhhhhhhhhhh??

A: I'll pick you up tomorrow evening at eight, darling.

Wear something revealing. And don't forget—I'm
very generou$$$!

[The dollar signs are mine, but you could practically hear them hissing on his snakey tongue.]

Then he left, and as soon as he was gone, Ümlaut stormed over to the counter to convince Raven she wasn't going to date his creepy friend. I'm NOT writing down their conversation. It was extremely tiresome and full of "Uhhhhhhhhh . . ." (Raven) and "Blood and Gor!" (Ümlaut). Here's what I picked up between naps:

1. Ümlaut has a terrible crush on Raven.
2. Attikol always goes for ladies Ümlaut has crushes on.
3. All the dolls in Attikol's show are modeled after real ladies he has known.
4. This one time, Attikol filled all the waterways of Venice, Italy, with bubble bath just because this one lady dared him to.
5. This other time, Attikol had the streets of San Francisco rearranged just so this other lady's favorite show The Streets of San Francisco would be more accurate.
6. This other other time, Attikol paid a sheik-ton of money to hold a fake Super Bowl just so he could make Ümlaut think his team had lost.
7. And once, Attikol paid a team of Nobel Prize–winning scientists to create a new kind of whoopie cushion to

embarrass Ümlaut in front of his lady friends.

8. For supposedly being friends, Attikol and Ümlaut seem to hate each other's guts an awful lot.
9. Attikol likes recreational straitjacketing, volcano diving, and cement boots (on other people).
10. Attikol has this bad habit of making life difficult for people who cross him, which is why Ümlaut can never keep a girlfriend and has had both his kneecaps broken.
11. Attikol also has a huge ego, which is his main weak spot.
12. Raven can buy some Attikol-free time if she can give him a challenge that's super hard (or just very time-consuming).
13. I do not care about this drama even just one little bit, but the challenge of coming up with a challenge for Attikol sounds pretty fun.

Day 6

Am feeling extremely peeved that I did not pay more attention to the stupid street-sweeping schedule. My lean-to has received an $86 ticket for being "parked" in a street-sweeping zone. Grrr!

Went back to the bus depot and tried to talk myself into picking a new town, but Myself reminded me that if I go, I'll be leaving behind not only $243 in tickets and some fairly annoying people, but any clues to my identity that might exist.

Will try to stick it out here a while longer.

Am not pleased.

Later

OK—something pretty odd just happened here at the mini-park. Had been feeling very motivated to figure out who I am and what happened to me so I can leave this ridiculous town forever. Decided to retrace my steps, try to jolt my memory a bit. Stood around in front of the El Dungeon for a while and then walked up and down the streets, checking the scene. Eventually ended up at the minipark. I was sitting on the bench, completely bored, and thought I'd practice my aim with the ol' slingshot. There were still plenty of lovely shooting rocks under the bench. Dead ahead from where I sat was the solo tree, and about five feet up the trunk I noticed this knothole. I aimed, and got it solid on the first shot. And then I heard this click from the bench. I turned around to see that one of the brass letters on the plaque, the "d" in "LeStrande," was now pushed forward just a little bit.

Weird! I ran my fingers around it, tried to pull it out, then gave it a little push, and the thing flipped upside down . . . and became a "g." Huh. It was . . . kind of le strange.

Spent about an hour shooting rocks at pretty much everything else in the park, but nothing else happened. Am excited to poke around town more and see what other weird surprises I can find. More secret doors concealed in wood paneling, for example. Mysterious SCHNEIDER door possibly hiding . . . I don't know, fascinating "Schneider"-related treasures. Portals to other dimensions. Bizarre elaborate chain-reaction contraptions that have waited centuries for me to come along and trigger them. YESSSSS!

If only!

Later—walking around town some more

Noticed four police officers standing around getting this dog to catch and eat wadded-up money. Once they had used up their small bills they moved up to twenties. Amazing.

Saw a loooong line of people waiting to get inside City Hall. Um, by "loooong," I mean twenty-three people. Hey, that must be at least half the Blackrock population. Did not really want to make eye contact with any of them, let alone have a conversation, but curiosity was kind of killing me. Asked some lady what they were all doing and she said it was ticket-paying day and everyone was waiting in line to pay various tickets and fines. Pretty much the most soul-crushing thing I've heard all day.

People are still giving me suspicious glares. Wish I knew why. Wonder if it was because I had four black cats following me.

Some lady tried to hand me a flyer encouraging Blackrock

citizens to have their phones charged up for St. Clare's Day. Told her no thanks since I have no phone. Her face showed Pure Horror.

Happened to be walking by the junk-mail factory in time to see Sizzle, Petal, and Grapey ending their day shift, to be replaced by HamHawk, Hurk, and Steve beginning the evening shift.

Am noticing that no one else in Blackrock looks like the people in the medicine show. Why do they even come here?

No one else in ANY small town looks like Raven. What's she doing here?

DITTO ME.

Later—back at the minipark, AGAIN

Found another cat collar like the one that said "Miles," this one for "NeeChee." It was under the bench at the minipark, snagged on the bottom of the seat, and impossible to see unless you were actually lying on your back under the bench, pretending it was an antigravity machine, which I kind of happened to be doing. Will see if Nitzer, Cabbage, or McFreely answers to "NeeChee."

Later

Back at the El Dungeon. Am still grinning (inside) about the funny stuff that just went down.

Attikol came to pick up Raven for her date—reeking of the same brutal cologne Ümlaut wears. He was all "Raven, dahling . . ." and I was all snorting, and Raven was all silent and pointing at me. So I told him his challenge, nice and loud in front of everyone, how he would have to move all the buildings in Blackrock one inch to the east before she would go out with him. You should have seen his face. It got all fake-sad and understanding, but you could tell he was irked. "You've been listening to Ümlaut," he said. "Don't listen to Ümlaut, he's jealous of his own codpiece! He's just a boy, Raven. You need a man. You need ME."

But Raven shook her head and crouched down under her cape, and Attikol took off to go lean on buildings, or something. Then we could laugh at him all we wanted.

Later

I have the four black cats to thank for helping me come up with that challenge while I slept. Here's what I dreamed: I was hanging out with the cats in the alley. One of them—Nitzer, the one with six toes and the white stripes on his tail—was staring at me really strangely, and then he put his front paws up on my refrigerator box and shoved it

The lean-to as I dreamed it. Raven's wig.

over an inch. Then he meowed, and I understood him! He was telling me to look underneath. I lifted it up a bit, and all this black hair came up from a hole in the ground under my lean-to. It was pretty gross, but I wasn't scared; I knew it was just Raven's wig. Then we walked around town and the cats did the same thing to a bunch of other buildings. All of them had different stuff under them: squid ink, crude oil, chocolate pudding, espresso, molasses... Finally we ended up right back at the El Dungeon. But they didn't move it, and that's how I knew what the challenge had to be. Pretty cool, actually, that Attikol really went for it. When he's done, I want to walk around town to see what was under all those buildings.

Later

You know, that Curls is kind of a rapscallion. He followed me out back to the alley and stood around chatting about nothing and preventing me from going peacefully into my refrigerator box. Luckily it's well disguised, so I don't think he knows I live in it.

Eventually, since Curls clearly wasn't going anywhere, I left. For lack of anywhere better to go, I ended up at Jakey's trailer. First thing he said, after "Hi," was "Baby cat? Kitten." Had to slap my forehead in disgust and relief.

ME: Thanks, man. Thought I was losing my mind.

JAKEY: I don't think you need to worry. You know a lot of stuff about the world that most people don't.

ME: [Getting very interested.] Really? Like what?

J: Like . . . uh, calculating terminal velocity. Whatever that is.

ME: Oh, come on. That's baby stuff. All you do is multiply the mass of the object by the gravitational acceleration at the Earth's surface, double that, divide by the drag coefficient . . .

J: Jeez, listen to yourself. Seriously, I bet you're the only person in Blackrock who knows that.

ME: Huh. OK. If you say so.

Weird, huh?

Anyway. Played some video games, taught Jakey's parrot some new words, and entertained each other swapping gossip about Ümlaut and Attikol. Yeah, the kid is all right, I guess. As long as there's nothing embarrassing in my mind.

Very Much Later

I'm finally back in my lean-to. And man, things may be tough right now, but in a way, I got it good. I got cats everywhere, a sandwich, a black cherry soda, my notebook. I got a skylight I can see the stars through, and the night air is perfect.

Belgium, I just realized I call soda soda and not pop. And haven't I heard the Blackrock locals asking Raven for pop? I could be way off—but I think people usually say one OR the other, depending on where they're from. And it definitely sounds hilarious to me to hear the Blackrock folk asking for pop.

Man, I must be desperate for clues. But still.

Later

I JUST remembered the cat collar I found earlier today at the minipark. I took it out and showed it to the cats. "NeeChee?" I said, and one of them (the one I called Nitzer) stepped up and meowed! I put it on him. Fit really well. What do you know.

NeeChee

Still Later

Went out for a late-late-late-night walk and guess what? I WAS FOLLOWED. This is amazing. The guy tailed me and the cats for about six blocks. Then we doubled back, got behind him, waited until he was lost, snuck back around in front of him, and popped out in his face in a dark alley, making him scream like a little boy.

Here's what he had to say for himself:

GUY: AIEEEE! Oh. My. You gave me a turn. I sure didn't see you standing there in the dark.

ME: What were you doing following me?

G: Excuse me. I work for the school board. I just

67

wanted to make sure you were safe walking around alone at night.

ME: OK, that's completely creepy, guy. Why don't you get lost.

G: Sorry. Yeah, it is creepy. Real sorry. Um, I'm actually the truant officer, Mr. Schneider.

ME: Oh, SCHNEIDER. [Giving up hope of mysterious fascinating "Schneider"-related treasures.] I guess you live upstairs from me?

S: Huh? Er, no, I mean, my grandmother lives upstairs from the El Dungeon, if that's what you mean.

ME: Very well, carry on.

S: [Obviously annoyed that I am giving him permission to talk.] I've been notified by the police that a 13-year-old has been roaming the streets unsupervised. And I'm afraid you'll have to report to school tomorrow.

ME: Oh, I'm IN school.

S: Uh-huh. And ... do you have any followup comments to that?

ME: ... I'm ... homeschooling ... myself? And ... I'm taking myself ... on a field trip.

S: Right, so. I'll see you in the morning, then, to escort you to LeStrande Comprehensive School. Meet you at the refrigerator box at eight.

DOUBLEBRICKING GOBFARX! Not happy about this.

Day 7

Was woken up at broad daylight o'clock by a tapping on the fridge box. Schneider was standing outside as promised. I'm sure I was looking grumpy. Had to block out the sun with my arm.

SCHNEIDER: Not a morning person?

ME: Not a daytime person.

S: I see.

[Then we walked in silence to LeStrande Comprehensive. Once we were there, though, I kind of freaked out.]

ME: Listen, Schneider. I really don't know what to tell these people. I found myself here six days ago with total amnesia. I don't even know my name.

S: You're kidding. Why haven't you asked the police for help?

ME: [No comment.]

S: Right. Never mind. OK, look, I'll do the talking.

And he was actually pretty good. He told them my name was Earwig Dungeon; Raven Dungeon was my mother; I'd just moved here from Wichita, Kansas; and I'd had a hard time recently and didn't want to talk about myself. And that was that.

Later

BLOGYAM!!! Have got to get out of here. Am writing this in the teachers' bathroom. Had to sneak in here since the regular bathroom is guarded. This place is insane. More later.

ABOUT TWENTY MILLION YEARS LATER

Have been released and am on my way back to the El Dungeon. Stopped off at the minipark because I am not ready to face human beings. Am completely traumatized. Was not able to write all day due to tyranny of maniac teachers. They were not happy with me. To say the least. Apparently, I even BREATHE the wrong way, in addition to every other little thing about me being WRONG and STRANGE. Will gnaw off a limb before I go back to that place.

I was mistaken about Schneider helping me out. Telling them my name was Earwig Dungeon pretty much killed my chances of escaping notice. As soon as he left, my first teacher told me I would never be known as Earwig in her classroom and that my new name was Charlene. Charlene Ellsbree.

TEACHER: Charlene, would you like to stand at the chalkboard and tell the class about yourself?

ME: No thanks. My name is Earwig.

T: Charlene, would you like to stay an hour after school scraping gum off desks?

[I stood at the chalkboard and told them all about myself.]

ME: My name is Earwig Dungeon. I come from Wichita, Kansas. My mom and I used to own a restaurant where we served human flesh. It was very popular. We were millionaires. I had a pony and a yacht. Now we are on the run from the FBI . . .

Received double detention for smart mouth.

It went on like this all day, with each teacher giving me a new name, threatening me with hard labor, forcing me to reinvent the story of my life, making good on their threats of hard labor, etc. Luckily there were only five teachers, and they each picked a different type of hard labor, so I'll have variety. Not that I am serving a minute of their detentions, because once I get to my fridge box, I am never coming out of it again.

Later

They have destroyed my fridge box. This town and I are finished.

Later

Am sitting on the bus to Wichita, Kansas. Ümlaut gave me the money. Probably to impress Raven with

The ex lean-to.

his gallant manners. He's not that bad, if you overlook his cologne, and everything else about him, except for the fact that he gave me the money.

Am sooooooooooooo glad to be rid of that ridiculous town, their floods of junk mail, their tickets and detentions.

Later—finally evening on the longest day of my life

Still on the bus. Bored out of my mind. Just now I was actually wishing for a little extra shot of amnesia so I could play hangman with myself. GUH!

An incredibly long time later

I don't think I like the segment of the population that rides the Red Rabbit bus line from town to town. Let me give you just a little sample of the conversational highlights so far:

"So I sez to her I sez, just you hand over that Slim Jim, and THEN maybe I'll give the baby back."

. . .

"Yeah so I ended up runnin' away from the army, but I kept the rifle, cuz hey, nice rifle."

. . .

"You *@!%ing kids shut up back there

ANARCHIP LUVIAN

Bored bohred borred board boored.

or I'll %&*ing *&%! your @&%$ to kingdom come or my
name isn't Sofronia Peabody Chucklebottom."

. . .

"Well, so Cousin Loretta tole me she's gonna have a Mickey
Mouse–themed wedding. I mean she's gonna have a little Minnie
and Mickey on her wedding cake and everything. So I axed her,
'Well, Cousin Loretta, are you and LeJim gonna wear Mickey
Mouse ears at the ceremony too?' And she said, 'Aw, Cousin Jill,
come on. I am NOT that EXTREME!'"

Have been giving evil death glares to anyone that passes my seat,
but unfortunately for me I now have a talkative seat-neighbor, this
middle-aged normal guy with that middle-aged, normal, serial-
killer look to him. I did my best to cut off conversation early.

NORMAL GUY:	[Finally wrapping up a long explanation of his business in Wichita.] So, what are you doing, riding the Red Rabbit all by your-self?
ME:	Sorry, I don't speak English.
NG:	What? You sound like you speak English.
ME:	Nope. I don't speak a word of English, and also, I have a speech defect, so if you don't mind, I'm going to sleep now.

Later

Bus Dream: I'm locked in the Blackrock jail. All the police are standing around laughing, eating doughnuts, polishing their guns, polishing their guns with half-eaten doughnuts, you know, police stuff. I keep asking why I'm locked up and no one hears me. I realize they are too stupid to build a jail cell that I can't break out of, so even though they can see everything I'm doing, I start looking over the whole cell inch by inch to find the way out. It takes forever. I inspect the door and windows 923 times, but there is no way I can jimmy them. I keep looking . . . every inch of floor, walls, I even crawl upside down over the ceiling . . . FINALLY I get to the toilet. Super-yuk, but I see something hidden down in it . . . I ask one of the officers for his shirt. He is dumb enough to take it off and hand it to me through the bars. I wrap it around my hand and reach down, down, down into dark water and there I feel a little switch . . . I push it, the gate opens, and I walk out. No one even looks at me, not even the officer who gave me the shirt.

Pretty good dream, but even that didn't cheer me up.

Later. So . . . Much . . . Later

Things to do when I get to Wichita:

    1. Look for posters with my face on them.

    2. Walk around aimlessly and hope someone recognizes me.

    3. Ask for free food.

    4. Make new lean-to.

5. Look for posters . . . yeah.
6. Um.
7.
8.
9. Um.
10.
11.
12.

13. I really have no desire to go to Wichita.

Blackrock may be a wretched little town, but it's the only place I have any memories of. That's tough to beat.

Later

I do not remember the word for that thing you use to make bread dark and crispy. I believe it starts with a D. (???) I don't care what Jakey says, I am clearly losing my mind.

On the bright side, I still remember how to say "Life sucks."

Day 8

Finally got off the bus in Wichita, in the late late hours of the night, extremely hungry, completely stiff and sore, freezing my bum off without any sleeves, and not happy about having to fig-ure out AGAIN where to eat and sleep in a town where I know no one and nothing. So it didn't come as a complete disappointment to hear Schneider yelling "EARWIG!" from across the street.

I still ran the other way. He caught up to me.

"Let's be reasonable, huh, kid? Look, why don't we get a snack and talk it over? I think it's all going to work out just fine! Huh? I bet you're hungry? Hey?"

He had me there. I let him buy me some sandwiches and listened to him chatter. Here's what I learned:

1. The police and the school are peeved about the $243 in tickets and the forty million hours in detention I owe them. Which is why they got Schneider on the case.

2. Schneider is actually a licensed private investigator, which is how he convinced the bus depot lady to tell him what city I'd bought a ticket to.

3. Schneider thinks it's a real shame the teachers insisted on calling me Charlene when Earwig is SUCH a coooool name.

4. Schneider thinks cats are the best animals EVER and soooo much cooler than dogs!

5. Schneider thinks it's soooooooooo unfair to hassle me for unlicensed slingshot use because slingshots are, like, really coooool. And stuff.

6. Schneider is so full of manure his hair stinks.

7. Schneider also happens to know quite a lot of interesting information, such as the fact that Ümlaut is paying the police to agree that Curls does not need to attend school.

8. Schneider also knows that Raven went into hysterics when Ümlaut told her he had paid for my bus ticket out of town. Now both Ümlaut and Attikol are freaking out and competing to see who can find me first so that they can win her LOVE. (Retch.)

9. Schneider agrees with me that I can turn this to my advantage if I want to go back to Blackrock.

10. Schneider admits there is some reward money in it for him from BOTH Attikol and Ümlaut if he brings me back to Blackrock.

11. Schneider looked very uncomfortable when I wondered out loud how Attikol and Ümlaut would feel if they knew he had made deals with both of them.

12. Schneider reluctantly compliments me on getting this information out of him and says I would make a totally wicked private investigator.

13. Schneider agrees to give me a cut of the reward money and to never use teen slang again if I come back to Blackrock with him.

Which is why I'm writing all this in Schneider's car on the way back to Blackrock.

Later—back in Blackrock

Life is way better in Blackrock when you have A) a beautiful bird-brain who relies on you to deal with her junk mail and keep her espresso machine running; B) two rich jerks willing to pay any money to keep the birdbrain happy; and C) a PI who is worried you will tell certain rich jerks that he is a shameless double-crosser. Attikol and Ümlaut have paid off my tickets and "convinced" the school to drop my detention. Schneider has agreed to do some detective work for me, beginning with a search of missing persons. And I now have a permanent permit to park my new fridge box in the back alley, regardless of the street-sweeping schedule. Still dealing with floods of junk mail, but at least things are looking up.

Later

Have been walking around town just to make sure no new MISSING posters with my face on them have appeared. Nada.

Spied on Attikol eating lunch with a bunch of important-looking people for a few minutes before I almost passed out with boredom. He had better start spending his time pushing buildings to the east if he really cares about getting a date with Raven!

Later

Cabbage came home to the lean-to this evening looking different somehow. I finally figured out that the bandage is off his shredded ear, and there are stitches in it! Who would have done that? Maybe I should track down the local vets? Will have to write more later as the cats are all yammering at me to come with them for our nightly exploration.

I wonder if they missed me like I missed them?

51916 IBC

Later

Excellent discovery tonight!! Those cats are goooooooooood! Right away when we got out of the fridge box they had a plan. They started leading me again, back to the spot where the security officer surprised me that one time. Except they were approaching from a roundabout way. So smart—we made it to the destination without interference. The destination turned out to be an auto impound lot surrounded with ten-foot razor wire. All four of them went up to this one spot in the fence and meowed. I was like, what? But then I saw they were sort of scratching under it. And actually, the dirt was pretty loose there, so we were able to squirm under without much problem.

I had no idea what we were doing there. But I kept following them.

I followed them through the rows of cars to one that stood out: the strangest and most beautiful van ever. I think it started out as a '63 VW van, but had mostly transformed into a bizarre and complicated contraption that looked like a science lab, rocketship, and botanical garden. And that's just what I could see from outside. The doors were chained and padlocked, and that's all I could really discover before the guard showed up with his flashlight and dog, and the cats all bailed. Just got a Polaroid and the license plate before splitting (see above and below). Will get Schneider on this tomorrow. Am half-expecting that he will have already found out who I am with his missing persons search. Fingers crossed.

the Amazing Van!

Day 9

Back to sleeping days. Up all night and it feels so right.

Met Schneider at the minipark. He says there are no missing persons that match my description. Terrible news, but he says not to let it worry me and that other leads are bound to turn up. Gave him my list of questions for him to research:

1. Owner of mystery van, license plate 51916 IBC?
2. Story of mystery van—Why was it impounded and when?
3. What happened to Rachel, former employee of the El Dungeon?
4. Background check on Raven—How does she run a business when she can't even complete a sentence? Seriously, who hired her?
5. Has she spent time in institutional learning facilities?
6. Background check on Attikol—How did he get his money, does he have a criminal record, etc.?
7. Where is the black rock this town is named after?
8. What's with all the beige paint?
9. And all the tree stumps?
10. Is there a veterinarian in Blackrock and can I get the address?
11. Any news on buildings getting shifted one inch to the east?
12. Did Rachel have any teenage daughters?
13. How long does it take to get over amnesia?

Also told him my current theory, which admittedly needs work: Rachel is actually my mother and the owner of that amazing van. Raven is her mentally challenged, beautiful, extremely evil twin sister. I had been living with my father in another town until his sudden, tragic death, when I came here to live with my mother. Meanwhile, Raven killed Rachel so she could take over the El Dungeon and . . . be . . . popular?? (OK. Motive needs work. No telling why anyone would want to take over the El Dungeon.) (Also, no telling why I think they would be twins . . . Did I see a movie with this plot, or what? Naturally I don't remember.) When I arrived, Raven tried to kill me. (See illustration of my bruises on Day 1. Obviously souvenirs of some kind of foul play!) But I survived and only lost my memories. Now that the residents of Blackrock have seen me around, she's playing nice until she gets another chance to get me out of the way.

Schneider took notes and said it showed a lot of imagination. He also asked me where I thought Attikol fit in. Actually, I don't think he fits in at all; I just want to know his story in case there's anything I can use to embarrass him.

And the black rock, well, that's just pure idle curiosity. Schneider said he assumed the town's founder, Emma LeStrande, gave the town that name, and he didn't know why. Probably some personal reason. He suggested that I might enjoy going down to the library and checking out their extensive collection of historical documents on her. I'd rather watch milk sour.

Later

It takes forever for milk to sour, even when you are encouraging it with all the power of your mind.

As a sort of side benefit to trying to watch milk sour, I ended up spying on Raven for many hours. She does very little unless people are placing espresso orders. It's hard to imagine her plotting to kill a fly, let alone a person. But she's suspicious as hell, all right. For one thing, she never sleeps. At least I can't figure out when she sleeps. Or eats—I've never seen her eat a thing. She doesn't drink coffee. And if no one's talking to her, her eyes get unfocused and you can practically watch her shutting down. I think she's up to no good, for sure. I wonder if it's worthwhile to check out her "secret" back room? Ehhh... Maybe if she weren't sitting in front of it 24/7. Zang, too bad she's NOT going on that date with Attikol.

Later

Typical evening at the El Dungeon. Ümlaut flirting with Raven, Curls trying to impress Ümlaut, HamHawk trying to keep his chess pieces away from Ümlaut's friends, Ümlaut's friends playing Calamity Poker (and all the swearing and acrobatics that go along with that), chairs breaking the front windows, police stopping by for their nightly payoff from Ümlaut . . . yep, not much interesting going on. Sorted another huge pile of junk mail, swept the floor, gave espresso machine a tune-up. Will report back if anything worthwhile happens.

Later

Spied on Raven until around one in the morning, then the cats and I went back to the impound yard. I had brought a piece of wire, a toothpick, and a hairpin, which I thought might be helpful in picking those locks.

They WERE helpful. How did I learn to pick locks? Interesting.

Inside, the van was a little disappointing. There were tubes and wires and stuff everywhere, but it looked to me like they were just for show. So it's an art car. Not a mobile laboratory. But still, pretty cool.

Hunted all over the van looking for clues and was just about to give up when I remembered to look under the seats. I was feeling around under the driver's seat when I found something metal that felt like a lever, so I pulled it, and there was this unlatching sound, and a little hidden compartment clicked open in the side of the van. Sweet! And inside was a cat collar like Miles's and NeeChee's with a tag for "Sabbath"! Asked the cats, and sure enough, the one with the shredded ear, the Cat Formerly Known as Cabbage, answers to "Sabbath"! I put the collar on him. This is GOOD stuff—a solid link between the van and the cats! I bet the van and the cats were Rachel's.

84

Sabbath

And that makes it even more likely she didn't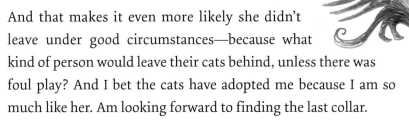
leave under good circumstances—because what
kind of person would leave their cats behind, unless there was
foul play? And I bet the cats have adopted me because I am so
much like her. Am looking forward to finding the last collar.

I found one other thing in the van worth writing about. I think
it pretty much confirms my theory that Raven is a cold-blooded
murderer who killed Rachel, my mother, most likely after a
riproaring, hairpulling struggle inside the van.

It's a chunk of her wig.

Very, very late, or early, depending on how you look at it

Hung out at Jakey's and didn't leave until around dawn. He has
this game called Brats Blow Chunks that we both just had to beat.
It took a while.

Hadn't seen him since my ordeals with Police and School. It
was kind of nice how, when he first saw me, he looked worried for
about a second, and then he just started laughing.

JAKEY: You ran a restaurant that served human flesh?
ME: [Laughing.] Good one, huh?
J: No wonder you got 40 years of detention.
ME: Yeah, well, just wait till I get my revenge.
J: I think you already did.

ME: What are you talking about?

J: Come on, you know it yourself. You won, and those people will never get over it.

ME: [Getting very interested.] That's what I was hoping. I mean, it was kind of cheating to have Attikol buy my way out. It's almost like admitting I was guilty in the first place.

J: Well, that's not how they see it. I think they just lost their favorite victim.

ME: How do you know? You see them at the medicine show or something?

J: Oh yeah. Everyone in town shows up there sooner or later. Anyway, sad cases. Your teachers have been arguing with their goldfish, and writing them detention slips, and suspending them from extracurricular activities. And your favorite patrolman just bought

himself an entire case of Ümlaut's Pätented Pötion of Pöwer.

ME: Say no more. You've made me a very happy girl.

J: [Laughing.] By the way: toaster.

Day 10

Had an excellent creepy dream that involved flying around Blackrock like a bird. After I got tired of daredevil aerial stunts, I started looking around town for somewhere to land. I didn't want to land on anything painted beige; I knew that stuff was deadly. And wouldn't you know—I couldn't find anything not painted beige. Started getting really tired and anxious to find a place to land, even for a second, but I couldn't find the minipark tree, and the buildings started crowding together so that I couldn't even find the ground. Finally I got so exhausted I just dropped out of the sky onto this beige roof. Right away the paint licked up my legs and crawled up my body and over my face, all cold and sticky and beigelike, into my mouth and nose and eyes and ears, and it just smothered the life right out of me, which is when I woke up.

Realized as soon as I was awake that I haven't seen or heard any birds in Blackrock. How sad!

Later

Schneider came to see me at the Das El La Dungeon. Don't ever let me say that guy is useless. No one else in Blackrock would have given ME all this dirt. When I asked him how he got it, all he would say is, "Eh, I hang out at City Hall a lot." Whatever that means. Also, he's lived in Blackrock all his life. Anyway:

1. Owner of mystery van, license plate 51916 IBC?—
   No such license plate registered. Anywhere.
2. Story of mystery van? Why was it impounded and
   when?—It was found parked in the middle of an
   intersection with the engine running and was towed,
   10 days ago.
3. What happened to Rachel, former employee of the El
   Dungeon?—She's currently enjoying a cruise to Australia.
   (Riiiiiiiiiiiiiiiight. That's what Raven wants us to think!)
4. Background check on Raven—How does she run a
   business when she can't even complete a sentence?—
   No public records on Raven. No one he talked to knows
   her story. She doesn't own the El Dungeon; everyone
   in Blackrock knows that Emma LeStrande owns it.

—Naturally I thought this was odd. Didn't Emma LeStrande die a long time ago? Yes, Schneider said, she died 13 years ago, but no one knew where her will was. So the building is being held in trust, or something like that, until a will or an heir showed up. Anyway, back to the list:

5. Has Raven spent time in institutions—see question 4.
6. Background check on Attikol—His money came from his

family. Certainly not from his gun and doll show. No criminal record at all. No permanent address, either.

7. Story of beige paint—Schneider is not actually sure. He remembers it happening: He was around my age, and it was near the time that Emma LeStrande died. His current theory is that it was part of a project of the mayor's called "Brighten Up, Blackrock!" when they made all these "improvements," like installing new streetlamps all through town and putting planters full of artificial flowers in front of all the public buildings. Gahh!

8. Story of tree stumps—They were cut down a long time ago to prevent disease. As if that makes any sense. Schneider is not sure why the one at the minipark was left alone, but his guess is that no one could locate the owner of the plot (Emma LeStrande, that is) to give permission. Or to pay the tree cutter to do it.

9. Where is the black rock this town is named after?—Still no answer on this one. Schneider will keep nosing around.

10. Vets in Blackrock—Only one, and Schneider had the address for me. You'll never guess—it's the El Dungeon's address! And the vet is Schneider's grandma. Funneee!

11. Buildings shifting an inch to the east—Not exactly, but check THIS out: The buzz is that Attikol intends to BUY all the buildings in town, then pay construction crews to

move them. Wow, I knew he was rich, but that's ridiculous.

12. Rachel is (was?) childless.

13. How long does it take to get over amnesia?—Could be a day, or a lifetime. Great.

Later—back at the El Dungeon

Noticed that HamHawk has a mini Magic 8-Ball on his keychain, you know, the kind that tells your fortune. I borrowed it from him and I've been asking it questions. Here's what I got:

1. Is Raven a murderer? **My sources say no.**

2. Is Raven really the birdbrain I think she is? **It is decidedly so.**

3. Does Jakey know anything about my amnesia that he's not telling me? **Cannot predict now.**

4. Can I expect more hassling from police and school board? **Outlook good.**

5. Is my family looking for me? **Don't count on it.**

6. Will I ever find home? **As I see it, yes.**

7. Do the four black cats belong to Rachel? **My reply is no.**

8. Does the cool van belong to Rachel? **Very doubtful.**

9. Is Rachel really on a cruise to Australia? **Concentrate and ask again.**

10. Is Rachel alive? **Reply hazy, try again.**

11. Am I related to Rachel? **Outlook not so good.**

12. Have I found ANY clues to my real identity?
You may rely on it.

13. Am I on the wrong track? **Better not tell you now.**

Later

I just reread the above entry. Smubbing Mongo! I am consulting toys for advice. I am clearly desperate!!!!

Later

I don't think I believe a single thing that mini Magic 8-Ball had to say, and especially not answer #1! Just now, I was eating one of Raven's sandwiches and bit into a big old wad of tinfoil. OK, maybe it was accidental. And then again, maybe next time I eat one of Raven's sandwiches, I'll swallow a big chunk of broken glass. Or a hearty layer of rat poison. Or maybe I'll just start choking on a hunk of rotten cheese. Maybe Raven will "try" to give me the Heimlich, but she'll "accidentally" end up crushing my rib cage instead. Aieeeee! Am starting to terrify myself here. All I can think about now is those

Outlook not so good

times I've come back to the El Dungeon after sleuthing around the town, only to find Attikol whispering to Raven, and she'd look up at me, all guilty-like. What if she WANTS to date him, and hates me for giving him that dumb challenge in front of everyone, and she can't say it's OK if he can't do it because he is convinced it would destroy his manly reputation in town? What if she's only pretending to be dull in the brain so no one will suspect her of killing Rachel? What if she's getting nervous that my memory will return and I'll tell the police everything I know about her? What if Attikol hates me for giving him that impossible challenge and wants to see me sleep with the fishes tonight? WHY AM I GETTING HYSTERICAL? FORGET THAT, WHERE ARE MY PARENTS? I NEED OUT OF HERE NOW!!!

Later

I am in deep danger!

Could not stand another minute of the El Dungeon, so I went and knocked on Jakey's trailer and interrupted his video game. Good thing no one wants to share a trailer with him. I guess telling the whole caravan about his roommates' dreams worked pretty well for him.

I wasn't actually expecting anything useful from him, but I got something anyway: He confirmed that Attikol does not like me and has been thinking of a way to get me out of the picture so he'll have better luck with Raven.

ME: [Starting to sweat, heart thumping.]
         What do you mean, "get me out of the
         picture?" Are you trying to tell me he's going to kill
         me?

JAKEY: I don't know what he's planning. I haven't seen
         him in days.

ME: Why, what's he doing?

J: Take it easy. I heard he's been having lunch with
         the mayor, paying off the police, stuff like that.

ME: Oh Belgium! He's going to kill me!

J: Don't be stupid. He might pay someone to kill you,
         but he would never do it himself.

ME: OH . . . BRICKING . . . BELGIUM!!

PARROT: OH . . . BRICKING . . . BELGIUM!!

J: CALM DOWN, EVERYONE!

At that point I had to bail. Sun was coming up and I was feeling sort of disintegratey. Came back here to the lean-to and got under a big pile of cats. Am thinking again that I should get out of town. But I'm not looking forward to leaving these cats behind. And where am I going to go this time? Let's see, names of towns, names of towns . . . can't seem to remember any. SIGH. Will sleep on it and see what tomorrow brings.

Day 11

Dreamed that I was trapped under a big, heavy bed. Ugh!! All these dust bunnies were swarming around me, growing bigger and bigger, showing their fangs and rolling their red eyes. I kept barely squirming away from them before they could bite my face. The worst part was that I couldn't really lift my head or arms or legs, so it was almost like being squashed into two dimensions, and it was super spooky. Then I noticed my feet were tingling as if I were getting electric shocks. I thought maybe I could electrocute some of the dust bunnies, so I kicked off my shoes and used my toes to feel around. I found some bare wires, wrapped my toes around them, and took a deep breath as I got ready for a big shock . . . But when I brought the wires together, all that happened was that the bed lifted up and let me go, and all the bunnies turned back into dust again.

Later

So it's St. Clare's Day today. I wouldn't have known except I came into the El Dungeon and EVERYONE (except me and Raven) was on the phone. It's normally not like that in here. But people weren't having long conversations, either; they were dialing, leaving messages, hanging up, dialing.

ME: Flathering bogyarks, what happened?

RAVEN: Huuuhhh?

ME: Why's everyone on the phone? Did the White House blow up or something?

R: Uhhhhh . . . Iono?

ME: GAH. [Turning to HamHawk.] Why's everyone on the phone? What happened?

HAMHAWK: Hang on, I'm leaving voicemail. Hi, Mom. Just calling to wish you a happy St. Clare's Day. And to tell you that I love you. And to thank you for all you do for me. OK, uh, see you tonight at dinner. [Hanging up.] Nothing happened. It's St. Clare's Day.

ME: So, what, Clare is the patron saint of voicemail?

HH: She's the patron saint of phones, so no one is supposed to answer calls all day. Out of respect for her blessed sainthood.

ME: But you're all on the phone.

HH: Not answering calls, though. Just leaving voicemail.

Like that makes any sense. But I'll tell you what St. Clare's Day accomplishes. Everyone is on the phone ALL DAY calling everyone in their address book, leaving them affectionate voicemails, listening to their own voicemails, sending reply voicemails to people they are glad to hear from, leaving even longer followup voicemails in reply to THOSE replies, and, in short, using the phone WAY MORE than any of them do on a normal day. Way to mess up a good idea.

Later

It's been a pretty grim day so far. Can't imagine what could have caused that. Maybe spending my day watching everyone else leave affectionate voicemails for their loved ones. How come no one has reported me missing? Do I really believe Raven killed my mother? WHERE ARE MY PEOPLE? Cannot stop wondering if I will ever remember my name or see my home again. Am trying to stay positive.

Am trying to talk myself out of hopping a random bus out of Blackrock.

Trying reeeeeeeeally hard.

Top 13 things in Blackrock:
1. Buses out of Blackrock.
2. Picture of imaginary black rock in all the official signage.
3. Police log in daily paper full of comedy. Today there was only one entry: "Homeowner in the 200 block of Coal

Ave. reported someone had entered his home and stolen a 5-gallon glass jug full of coins. The only other thing missing was a swig of whiskey." I'm not kidding.

4. Sandwiches at the El Dungeon very tasty.
5. Police are easily bought off.
6. Local cats. Excellent!!!!
7. Lax security at auto impound lot.
8. Wastelands always visible in the distance.
9. Decent stars at night despite all the bright streetlamps.
10. Great Dumpster pickings.
11. School's . . . out . . . forever! (For me, anyway.)
12. Plenty of unused back alleys for slinking around in.
13. That cozy, private, incredibly well-designed lean-to behind the El Dungeon, and that cool girl who lives in it.

Later

!!!!!!HAVE FOUND OUT MY TRUE IDENTITY!!!!!!

Must breathe. Breeeeeeeathe.

Will start from the beginning.

Had been doing some spying on Curls, who was spending the evening sitting alone at his table, trying to look very busy with voicemail, and instead looking very foolish. It seemed to me like he was only pretending to celebrate St. Clare's Day like a local. I decided to go harass him a little.

ME: You aren't from around here, are you, boy?

CURLS: Chaaa, you know I'm not. Do you mind? I'm leaving voicemail.

ME: [Sitting down at his table.] How would I know that?

C: Hi, Ümlaut, it's me, Ripper. Hope you're, uh, having a great St. Clare's Day. I actually don't know if you celebrate St. Clare's Day or not. But if you do, Happy St. Clare's Day. Fffffwwwwhhhh. I'll, uh, see you later. [Hanging up.] You know, you're supposed to call everyone in your address book that you want to stay in your address book; otherwise they get deleted.

ME: Why do they get deleted?

C: Oh, it's just town policy. To . . . save electricity.

ME: Do you actually believe all that?

C: [Looking angry, then spiteful.] Do you ALWAYS have to act like you're smarter than me, Molly? [And then he kind of mentally bit his tongue. But he saw he had no chance of a coverup, so he braved it out and gave me a "What are you gonna do about it?" look.]

ME: [Thinking fast. Pretending to know what he was talking about in hopes of getting further information.] Oh, so you think it's OK to call me Molly now?

C: [Looking chastised.] Sorry to blow your cover,

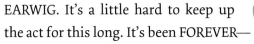

EARWIG. It's a little hard to keep up the act for this long. It's been FOREVER— I mean, like, two WEEKS since you rolled into town? I mean, this is the VERY first time you've broken character this WHOLE TIME. [Pausing. His voice shifting tone to Pal-Casual.] Did you get my voicemail?

ME: [Keeping a disinterested face.] I've lost my phone. [Long pauses as I fought back hysterical laughter.] That's why. I haven't left you. A St. Clare's voicemail.

C: [Long questioning stare.] Man, you are in DEEP this time, Molly. Are you . . . feeling OK?

ME: [BRITTLING FAVVWARX, he knows who I am and my name is Molly he knows me HE KNOWS ME.] [Laughing casually.] Well, you know, I have this pesky amnesia.

C: [Rolling his eyes. Making quotey fingers.] Oh, right, the "amnesia."

MEMOLLY: [Giving him my notebook, open to a blank page.] Just do me a favor and write down my parents' names and address, OK?

C: Huh? I don't know your parents.

MM: No time for that; give me your phone. What's my last name again?

C:	[Looking afraid, very afraid.] Merriweather.
MM:	[Dialing information, then City Hall; paging Schneider; requesting a meeting RIGHT AWAY so I can GO HOME!!!!!! Then handing Curls his phone again.] Good thing City Hall is still answering the phone. So, refresh my memory, Curls. Where'd we meet, again?
C:	[Looking aghast.] Uh, Toad Suck, Arkansas? Four years ago?
MM:	Man, so, we're, like, friends?
C:	Um, yes? You're the one who gave me my nick-name.
MM:	Yeah . . . Curls. Um, I know that.
C:	RIPPER.
MM:	Oh, right, man, Ripper, listen, I gotta catch you later, gotta meet someone . . . Thanks for letting me use your phone . . .

And I hustled out of there. Am now waiting for Schneider at the minipark. Cannot wait to tell him I would really, really appreciate it if he would locate the Merriweathers and tell them Molly needs to be picked up RIGHT AWAY AND THANK YOU VERY MUCH!

Later

My parents are on their way to Blackrock. I am dizzy with success and information. And espresso. Met Schneider at the minipark,

then sprinted back to the El Dungeon to interrogate Curls and collect my belongings.

Here is what I've been able to find out about ME, MOLLY MERRIWEATHER, from Schneider and Curls:

1. I live in Zigzag, Oregon!
2. My parents are George and Sharon Merriweather!
3. I'm an eighth grader at Gallmark Junior High School!
4. I have been reported missing (and subsequently found) three times in the past four years!
5. I'm not currently on the "missing" list, and Schneider has been promising to give my parents a hard time about that!
6. Curls says he hadn't seen me for about four months before I showed up here, but last time we were hanging out, some kooky old lady told us we would enjoy this town called Blackrock!
7. But Curls and I went our separate ways there in Turniptown, Pennsylvania!
8. And he came here by himself about three weeks ago!
9. And has been working on getting himself a job with the traveling medicine show ever since!
10. And was only a little surprised when I showed up nine days later, "pretending" to have severe amnesia!
11. He is also relieved that I am finally "out of character" so he can ask my advice about how he can get more popular with the Ümlauts!
12. I hate to think what #11 tells me about myself as a person!

13. I am starting to feel afraid, very afraid, of the reality of my parents, my home, my belongings, my IDENTITY, all of which are about to hit me, whether I am able to remember them or not, with great force, much like something traveling at huge speed would hit something else of unimaginable mass and density!

Later

Have reunited with my parents!!

I'm in their luxury sports utility vehicle and we're headed back home to Zigzag, Oregon. I should be more excited to be leaving Blackrock, but all I can think is: I never said goodbye to the cats. I never said goodbye to Jakey. I really hope Raven understood when I told her I was rescued and she should NOT have

George and Sharon

Ümlaut and Attikol pay Schneider to fetch me back. Really wish I had brought the cats with me. REALLY, REALLY, REALLY wish I had the cats.

—OK. Back to Sharon and George.

I started out with "Mom" and "Dad." But that just wasn't rolling off my tongue right. So they said it was OK for me to say Sharon and George while I still had the amnesia. They said I'd be going to a fancy specialist about the amnesia. They described my spacious, stylishly decorated bedroom and its entertainment system. They talked about the ponies. The ponies!!! I hope they're real. I hope there's at least the ponies.

I asked them if I had a yacht but they laughed and said oh no honey you don't have a yacht and it felt like it was the first time anyone had ever called me honey and it was GREAT.

Later

The drive home has wiped me out. Have been staring intensely at the passing landscape trying to recognize a landmark, or eliminate amnesia from my brain by force of imagination alone, or something. Saying "Molly" over and over in my mind. Asking Sharon dumb questions about my habits and preferences. ("Hey, Sharon, do I take baths or showers?" "Both, sweetheart.")

Can't wait to be home can't wait to be home can't wait

Next day—Tuesday

There are actually ponies. More on them later.

I slept in my own bed last night and let me tell you it was ALL RIGHT! Actually I had fallen asleep in the car on the way home, so

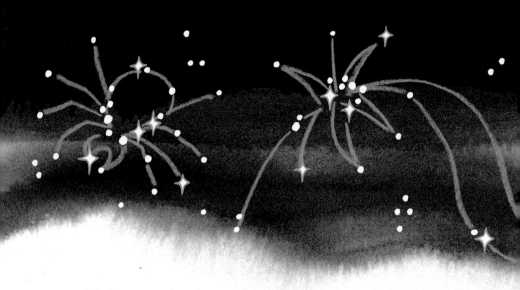

I didn't get to enjoy the approach to the house. Woke up just long enough to stagger inside and fall into bed, then gaze at the ceiling for a delicious minute, tracing the dreamy shapes in the plaster illuminated just a lick by the bluish moon; anticipating the day I'd have my memory back and could revisit the homegrown constellations I'd surely seen there and named in childhood. What would they be? The Dancing Tarantula? The Disbelievers' Chorus? The Party of Blackbirds? The Nettle's Tongue?

It felt like I slept about 100 miles deeper than I have in the past two weeks.

MUCH Later

Looking back, this one thing is obvious: Before I contacted my parents and told them to come get me, I should have asked myself

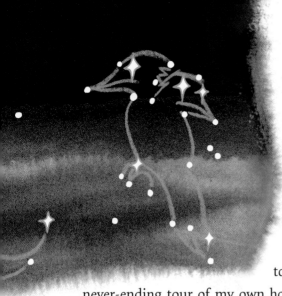

why I ran away in the first place.

My parents are nice, nice people, but awfully tiresome. They actually seem kind of excited about my amnesia, since it gives them a reason to torture me with a full-scale, never-ending tour of my own home in excruciating detail. Did you know that wooden floors hold up better to foot traffic if you rotate the runners every four months? Or that your rumpus room will stay perfectly tidy all year round if you keep it locked up tight? Or that Sherman's, downtown, does by far the most reliable job of framing family portraits in the most tasteful way possible?

Is it grossly self-centered of me just to want information on MYSELF?

We did eventually get to that, of course. The history of my life has been very well-documented in dozens of albums of photos, some home movie footage, and many crates of memorabilia. But I haven't had any quality alone time with that stuff, believe it, because Sharon and George thought it was more important to give me the guided tour of EVERY SINGLE OBJECT in my room:

"So, this bedframe, we bought you at Gooding's last March, to replace the last one that got nicked by your riding boots."

"And this jewelry box, we gave you that for your thirteenth birthday, and it came from Bick's, and so did your charm bracelet, but we gave you that when you were nine."

"And THIS sweater came from Four Daughters, and so did this dress and these pants, and most of your underwear."

. . . AND SO ON until I actually put my head down on the pillow and pretended to go to sleep. If tomorrow is anything like today, it may destroy me.

Later

Went and hung out with my ponies.

George told me their names were Tuffy and Tweety. When he saw the look on my face, he said, "Well, you named them when you were about five, if that makes you feel any better." It sure didn't.

Ponies are beautiful, intelligent creatures, you know, so it was all the more disappointing when they put their ears back and bared their teeth at me. George said they were probably just upset that I'd been gone. He got me saddled up for a ride on Tweety, and I felt like a dumb muppet up there, without a clue what to do. So I got a long and awkward riding lesson (because of which, by the way, I now have to put a pillow down before I sit!). "I thought horseback riding was one of those things, like riding a bike," I said to George. "You know,

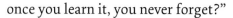

once you learn it, you never forget?"

He scratched his head. "Well, do you still know how to ride a bike?"

Turns out I do. Very well. SIGH. I will keep working on the ponies.

Later

Pretty boring day. I have a feeling that boring is normal here.

I do not understand my bedroom at all. Why is it so painfully tidy? It needs major reorganizing. Don't really feel like it at the moment, but maybe tomorrow. First thing, I think I'll hide away the trophies.

Later

I have serious concerns about how bad all of my music is. Have spent some time skimming through my collection of cardiofunk, yacht rock, arena boogaloo, heartland country, and frat rap. I can safely say that I now find all of this COMPLETELY UNLISTENABLE and will need an all-new music collection as soon as possible.

Wednesday

Met the housekeeper. I don't recognize him even one tiny little bit. Asked Sharon when I would be seeing the specialist and she said tomorrow. Worked on my riding skills even though my bum feels like it's made of fire and broken glass. Ponies are no longer baring their teeth at me, thanks to lots of apples and sugar cubes, but they also aren't galloping majestically toward me with their manes billowing out behind them when I go out to their corral. Instead, they look depressed and disappointed. Am doing what I can to cheer them up. Renamed them Bratwurst and Toulouse. Since I cannot work myself up to actually saying their former names out loud.

Sharon was full of hugs and sugary snack treats today. She also spent a lot of time staring at me with her forehead all wrinkled when she thought I wasn't looking. She sort of half-tried to persuade me to start wearing the clothes in my large, unfamiliar closet instead of this black dress I've been wearing since Blackrock. I did let her launder it, but I took a long bath while I waited. I don't know, I just feel funny putting on anything else. Will tell the shrink about that if he seems to be of any use.

I also spent some time with the top-of-the-line entertainment system in my room. I immediately saw the need for some minor improvements, and got it rewired within a few minutes. I know I could really get it sounding good if we just had a soldering iron, but apparently we DON'T. Which I really don't understand. I also don't understand why I haven't already customized the spit out of this stereo. It looks as clean and perfect as the day George and Sharon paid a huge heap of money for it. Ended up tuning the radio to static, which was better than nothing, and WAY better than Hoopy Jankers and the Goodtime Belly Bouncers. Who, I'm mortified to say, used to be my favorite band.

That's not the only thing in my room that I have issues with. Here's another good example: On my dresser there's this large framed photo of me with a big group of fun-looking people my age. Probably, like, twenty-three of my closest friends. My hair's in a different style and I'm wearing the most perky grin you ever did see. Obviously, I'm thoroughly enjoying myself. With that Big. Group. Of Fun-Looking. People.

Please tell me the camera was LYING!!!

Later

Have had some quality alone time with the photo albums, the home movies, and the crates of keepsakes and other documentation of my life history. I don't know if I feel like writing any of it down. I mean, what it adds up to is: I was born. I grew some teeth, lost them, grew some more. I've spent time in school. I have relatives, friends—lots of friends—and ponies. I've been to Disneyland. Etc. Etc. Etc. I think the most informative . . . uh, information about myself came from my school yearbooks. Each one must have been signed by the entire student body and most of the faculty. I read through all the messages people wrote to me over the years and here are a few representative entries:

molly· you have the "best hair" & the "best clothes" it's too bad you didn't win "best hair" or "best clothes" but i guess "most popular" & "most athletic" were pretty good & someday we'll be partying with "prince william" on his yacht & look back on these days & laugh & laugh & if there was one girl in this school that "had it all" it would be you so "be good" & see you in honors history! ♡
YM BFF!

Hay Molly you are the best I can't wait till next year! We are going to rule the school just you wait!!! Can I come over and borrow everything you wear?? Oh yeah and you have the best bedroom and the cutest ponies EVAR can I have them? J/K!! Never forget "Take a booger, leave a booger" and Mr. Pick in Purple!!! Also – Friends are kisses blown to us by angels. KEEP IN TOUCH!!!!!!!!

WUSSUP MOLLY IT WUZ FUN BEING IN ENGLISH WIT U AND THANKS FOR LETTING ME COPY UR TESTS U ROCK AND SWIM TEAM WUZ ROCKIN U TOTTALLY WON US THE TITLE. SORRY I ALWAYS BORROWED MONEY OFF U BUT THANKS FOR BEING GENERUSS AND I'LL PAY U BACK SOMEDAY WHEN I'M RICH LIKE U LOL!! ANYWAY THANKS FOR BEING A TITE FRIEND AND I'LL CATCH U LATER!!

OMES CORP.
O BOX

Dear Molly, It was a pleasure having you in three of my classes this year. You have a bright and promising future ahead of you. I fully expect to see you bring home Olympic gold someday. Best wishes from Mr. Ito.

It appears as though I ~~was~~ am a rich, popular, well-dressed girl who keeps a neat bedroom and wins trophies at everything she does. But I can't say that any of this seems familiar to me. Let alone flattering.

Thursday

Losing my will to write regular entries. What's the point? The shrink says he will have me cured of amnesia in three days, tops. Waste of time to keep writing . . . it's just a habit that I'll soon be over.

A lot later

Not over the habit quite yet. In fact I feel like dwelling on my memories of Blackrock. It's such a novelty for me to have MEMORIES of anything. I've been thinking about the day I came back to the El Dungeon with Schneider after Wichita, and both Attikol and Ümlaut tried to take credit for bringing me back, and Raven had already forgotten she ever missed me. Ahahahha hah ahha. And the time Schneider was asking my parents why I hadn't been reported missing. "Well, this was the eighth time, and she always came back on her own . . ." Weirdos. And that time Attikol asked Raven if she would let him romp through her hair some moonlit night, and Raven was all, "Uhhhhhhhhhhhhh . . . no?" HAHAHA! And that especially rowdy game of Calamity Poker when Attikol challenged Ümlaut to recite Shakespeare's Sonnet 18 . . . in Morse Code. "Deeet

de deeet deeet deeet de de deeet de de de de deeet . . ."
And most of all: finding the cat collars and learning Miles', NeeChee's, and Sabbath's real names. McFreely's real name will probably remain a mystery forever now. Belgium!

Oh, that reminds me. I never did go see Schneider's grandmother, the town vet, to ask if she had stitched up Sabbath's ear. Probably my only lead on the cats' real owner. Had a moment of sadness for whoever that person might be, because let me tell you, they are missing some goooooood cats.

Then had an hour of sadness for myself, because I am also missing some gooooooood cats.

Much later

It's late, late, late. I snuck out and walked around downtown Zigzag for a long time looking for something familiar. If you can believe it, and this is kind of embarrassing, I almost had myself convinced that me being here was all a big mistake, and these nice people were just complete idiots who were mistaking me for their daughter. And then this kid on the opposite corner called my name, and I thought about how even I recognized myself in all those pictures, and I should just give it up and figure out how to be Molly. Anyway, I let the kid do the talking. Not that it made any sense. Something about a comic he was knitting? About this girl who made the ultimate sacrifice—for beets! Or something like that. And he asked me if I'd be meeting up with the others later and I said yeah but then I bailed on actually going. Maybe tomorrow. Not sure if I am actually interested in rejoining my extensive circle of well-dressed, chipper friends.

Not sure if I am actually interested in ANYTHING related to being Molly Merriweather.

Ehhhhhhhhhh.

Friday

Saw the shrink again today, but nothing about my former life is getting clearer. Shrink-man says to just give it time, and until I get my memory back, he will keep telling my parents I shouldn't go back to school yet. (Doesn't he realize that's really not good motivation?) He also says writing in this journal is counterproductive to my goal of regaining my identity, so this will probably be my last entry.

So I guess this is it. Bye, Dear Diary.

Whatever.

Later

There are doubts! There are serious doubts!

I hate to say it . . .

BUT

I may not be Molly Merriweather after all.

(!)

Things fell apart after dinner tonight when Sharon asked me what I wanted to drink with dessert, and I said black cherry soda, and she laughed and said, "There's orange pop in the fridge." POP!!! I am not from this household, I tell you. And if I had ever actually lived here, those ponies would know me.

ALSO: I don't recognize the taste of the air, the smell of the water, the kind of towels in the bathroom, the mac'n'cheese, the night sounds, "my" stuff, or "my" name.

Am feeling VERY confused. Not sure what to do. Am going to start with some straight talk with Sharon and George.

Later

Evidence pointing to me being Molly:

1. My old friend Curls thinks I'm Molly.
2. Sharon and George think I'm Molly.
3. Ditto our housekeeper, that kid I saw downtown, and the neighbors.
4. Lots of photographic evidence.
5. Leaving this boring place seems like something I'd do.
6. Ditto taking on fictional identities.
7. Molly is/was an animal lover. I can relate.
8. I am having a hard time beating any of the high scores on the video games in the house.
9. Molly has won 3 science fair trophies. Sounds like something I could do.
10. As for the popularity thing, Shrink-man says a change

in personality could happen after head trauma.

11. Sharon and George say we have no relatives my age at all, let alone any that look like me.

12. Extreme unlikeliness of ANYONE (relative or not) looking so much like me.

13. I SOMEHOW ended up in the same town as Curls. What are the odds?

Evidence that I'm not Molly:

1. Sharon and George agree that I seem different than normal.

2. They say I used to be a day person.

3. Pop vs. Soda.

4. Ponies do not know me.

5. I don't know how to ride the ponies. To be specific, my BODY doesn't know how to ride the ponies. My bum is still yelling at me about the pain.

6. Am horrified by thought of being popular. No desire to see my former friends.

7. Formerly candidate for winning Best Dressed; now I prefer to wear the same thing every day.

8. Though a winner of science fairs, Molly was not known as mechanical genius. Stereo still in dire need of

modifications. Toaster oven in kitchen needs a tune-up. Etc.

9. Sports lover. Ewwww.
10. Hoopy Jankers and the Goodtime Belly Bouncers. Ewwwwwwwwww.
11. My hair is in a different style in all those photos.
12. Bedroom seems way too tidy.
13. I just don't feel like Molly.

Still, I don't know if I can really BELIEVE that I'm not Molly Merriweather without further evidence.

For example . . . meeting Molly Merriweather face-to-face.

Will just have to go find her.

Much later

Waited until Sharon and George were asleep, then snuck out and walked around until I found that kid again who knew me, or thought he did. I asked him where everyone was and he said at the usual spot. I said let's go and I let him lead.

We got to this overpass where a bunch of scruffy-looking kids were hanging out and as we walked up, sure enough, they were all like "MOLLY!" and "Where have you been?" and stuff, but then, when I got into the light from the trash-can fires, they kind of got silent and were all staring at me, maybe because I still hadn't said a word, and then this one girl was like, "Hey, Molly—you seem . . .

different?" and I told them I was Molly's cousin and I was trying to find her, and then everyone had their story to tell:

1. Molly had, like, MAJOR problems with how boring her parents were.
2. Molly ran away, like, all the time.
3. Her parents never even freaked out when she left, as long as her grades were good.
4. Molly and I look SOOOOOOO much alike omigod!!!!!
5. Molly was, like, the BEST at making up her own funny lyrics to popular songs.

6. Everyone had an AKA that Molly gave them, but she would never let anyone give her a nickname.
7. But she would always invent a new, like, identity for herself whenever she bailed town.
8. Molly often handed out the big wads of cash her parents gave her.
9. Molly had these awesome ponies that she trained herself.
10. Molly (and everyone else in Zigzag) would say "pop" not "soda."
11. Molly was tight friends with this kid Ripper who had been running away since he was, like, six months old or something, and was a total pro at it, and the two of them knew runaways in just about every town in the country by now.
12. Molly was pretty much the most popular girl anyone knew.
13. No one knew where Molly was this time around, but this one girl said Molly always used to bust a gut over towns with funny names, so if SHE were looking for Molly, that's where she'd look.

It appears as though I was a rich, popular, well-dressed girl who kept a neat bedroom and hung out under the overpass at night with a bunch of runaways. Oh. Except I WASN'T.

Later

Went down to the local bus depot and searched the departure list for the town with the funniest name. Am now scheduled to leave for Monkey's Eyebrow, Arizona, in twenty-three minutes. Fingers crossed that my instinct is correct, and I find Molly under the first overpass I check.

Am reeeeeeeally hoping that I will soon know for sure whether A) I am not (and never have been) Molly Merriweather, or B) I used to be Molly Merriweather, but have lost all trace of my original personality due to pesky amnesia. [Shudder.]

Day 16

No Molly in Monkey's Eyebrow, though she (or I?) was here (going by "Tigra") about a year ago. After searching all the overpasses and talking to all the runaways (most of whom had stories to tell about the legendary Ripper), I took the next funny-town-name bus out of there, and am now on my way to Pflugerville, Texas. I can only hope that the runaway network there knows something. Anything.

Day 17

Nothing in Pflugerville. Have moved on. Am on the bus now to Willacoochee, Georgia. Wish me luck.

Day 18

All this travel and meeting strangers is crushing my spirit. Really miss those times in Blackrock when I would do a lot of silent communing with the cats as therapy. Am extremely sorry I don't have the cats with me.

Anyway, this kid in Willacoochee thought I was "Bunny," but had not seen me (Molly?) in about two years. Am on the bus

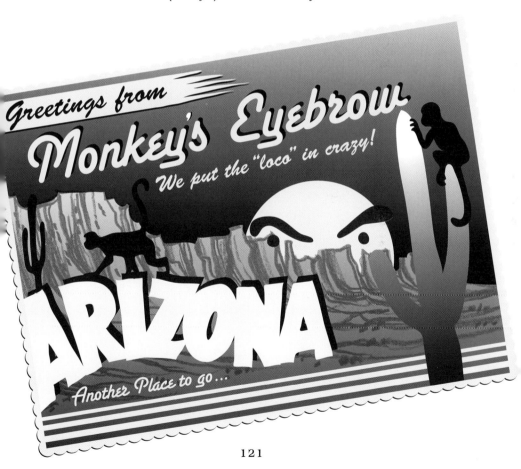

again, about an hour away from Sopchoppy, Florida. Could use a lucky break.

Later

Am sick to death of hitting one random town after another looking for Molly. Was "recognized" as "Squid" in Sopchoppy. I guess Molly was there about six months ago. Or I was. Hard to say who is who at this point. Maybe Tigra, Bunny, and Squid are separate people. Maybe there are even more of us. GAHHHH.

Later

Finally, a lead. Some kids on the bus recognized me (as "Yodi") and said they saw me in a town called Blandindulle just two weeks ago. Am on my way there now. Fingers crossed.

Day 20

HEY, AMNESIA GIRL!
YOU ARE NOT MOLLY MERRIWEATHER!

I had to tear out the stuff I wrote about what's going on. I CAN'T KNOW IT, this is very important. I just hope I can do . . . what I need to do . . . this time.

Later (same day???)

OK.

Here's what I know, take 2:

1. I've been sitting on this park bench for at least two hours.
2. I've got no actual memory of anything I've done before that. In my entire life.
3. I'm really glad to have this notebook full of information, which I've just read three times.
4. Based on my notebook and what I can see around me (e.g., the completely pointless ten-foot wrought-iron gate with no fence to go with it, and the plaque on the bench that says EMMA LeSTRANGE), I assume I'm back in Blackrock.
5. Something happened to me between Day 18 and Day 20 that gave me amnesia. Again.
6. No telling if I actually made it to Blandindulle or not.
7. No telling if I actually found Molly Merriweather or not.
8. No telling WHO I actually am, besides (obviously) being

129

Amnesia Girl. But I guess I'm not Molly Merriweather.

9. There's something I need to do in Blackrock that requires me to have amnesia.
10. In my pockets I found a slingshot, a pen, and some pieces of folded paper (pasted in below).
11. Certain people I've read about in this notebook are going to want explanations for why I'm back in Blackrock. Explanations that I better come up with.
12. I am going to need a new fridge box for tonight.
13. I have some cats to meet.

Here is the first piece of paper I found in my pocket:

I immediately unfolded
it and found this one:

IF THIS IS STILL
DAY 20,
YOU ARE NOT
IN ANY KIND
OF EMERGENCY!

I opened that one and found this one:

SERIOUSLY.
Do not open
until at least
Day ~~25~~ ~~26~~ 27!!!!....

So I guess I'll wait it out. Am not happy, though.

Later

These are some gooooooood cats, all right, but I don't have the tiniest memory of them.

Found a fridge box tucked away behind the Dumpster in the alley. Am hoping it was mine before and that the cozy slept-on spot was not made by some other homeless person. Am writing EARWIG on the inside of the doorflap in case of future attacks of amnesia.

Wish I could delay going into the El Dungeon but am starving. Do not want to talk to anyone. Hope I will recognize who is who. Hope I do not make too big a fool of myself.

Later

Am sitting in the El Dungeon eating the most excellent sandwich. CounterChick/Raven was very happy to see me. At least, I mean, she said "Uhhhhhhhh, hi" in a kind of lively way. Have not explained myself to anyone. Should probably track down this Schneider person and tell him the scoop, though.

Later

Am avoiding talking to anyone about anything. Am hiding behind the counter of the El Dungeon, staring at the regulars through my spyhole. Am pretty sure I recognize HamHawk by his chessboard and mini Magic 8-Ball, but I kind of have no clue about the rest, so I'm reassigning nicknames randomly. Have not seen anyone that could be Curls.

Later

In the interest of wasting time, I sorted a huge pile of junk mail for Raven and found a letter addressed to EARWIG! It was from my old fake mom, Sharon. Here's what she had to say:

Dear Earwig,

I'm really sorry you decided to leave us but I just wanted to write and tell you that I understand. I'm hoping you eventually go back to Blackrock so you get this letter. I didn't know where else I could send it.

I realize now that you are not Molly. It was your dress that really clinched it for me. Molly is a special girl but as far as I know, she does not have any dresses that can hold a laundry basket full of rocks and cans in the pockets.

If you happen to see her in your travels, tell her we love her and hope she is coming back soon.

I hope you regain your memory and find your real home. If you don't, you can always come back here.

Your "other" mom,
Sharon

P.S. George says hi too!

Zang, what a relief to know they won't be coming after me to take me back to Zigzag! Good point about the dress, too. Seems like I never really thought about that before. Will investigate carrying capacity of pockets when I feel up to it.

Later

Went out to the impound lot with the cats to check out that cool van I'd been reading about. No security in sight (probably doughnut break time), so I was able to pick the lock in peace. Then the cats and I settled down inside the van, which was even cooler than it seemed from what I'd written about it. I don't really know if I still think it's just an art car. For example: There's this crazy glass thing bolted to one of the side panels that, at first glance, you

might assume was just some kind of sculpture. But now I notice there's traces of chemicals on the inside, and scorch marks on the outside. So maybe the van actually IS some kind of mobile laboratory . . . and it's just kind of out of commission at the moment.

I also rediscovered the now-empty secret compartment where I found Sabbath's collar. I think I was right to assume that the cats and the van belong to the same person, since the upholstery seems to be made of about 45% man-made materials and 55% black cat hair, whiskers, and claw fragments. I guess I should be disgusted by that, but it seems kind of comforting. Took a looooong nap in there with cats piled on me. Good stuff.

Later

Was hanging out at the minipark when this man walked past, did a double take, and said, "Ear—Moll—Earwig? What are you doing back from Zigzag?"

ME:	Let me guess, you must be Schneider.
SCHNEIDER:	[Looking at me like I am on fire.] Ummm . . . you KNOW I am.
ME:	I do now.
S:	[Sitting down on the bench.] What happened?
ME:	Well. I somehow found out I'm not actually Molly Merriweather. And then I lost my memory again.
S:	Wow. Um . . . . bummer.

ME: For real.

S: [Long pause.] So, any leads?

ME: Nope. Well, I guess I'll go visit that vet, I mean, your grandma, and ask her if she's the one who stitched up Sabbath's ear. You know, maybe she knows something about his owner.

S: Good thinking! Great plan! You never know what one small lead can . . . uh, lead you to! Well, keep me posted on your progress!!!!

Man, was Schneider always such a spazzy cheerleader? All that encouragement seemed suspiciously over the top. Or maybe it's normal for him. I really have no idea. Since I essentially just met him a minute ago.

Amnesia, Part I was bad enough, but Amnesia, Part II is full-on loathsome.

Later

Decided it was a bit too late in the day to make a social call to Schneider's grandma, so instead I went to re-meet Jakey and apologize for not saying bye when I left to go be Molly. One nice thing about that kid is, if you ever need to apologize to him, you don't really need to do it out loud.

I apologized out loud, anyway. I thought it was better manners.

JAKEY:	Don't worry about it. Wow, you have a lot more in your mind these days. And . . . also a lot less. Too bad about Amnesia, Part II. Good thing you keep that notebook, huh.
ME:	Huh. Anything interesting?
J:	Eh, the ponies sound cool, but the rest of the Molly stuff is kind of . . . kind of not you.
ME:	Yeah. Pretty glad I turned out not to be her.
J:	What about your dress, though?
Me:	Huh?
J:	Don't you think it's kind of, uh, unusual that you could fit all that stuff in the pockets?
ME:	I guess.
J:	[Looking awkward.] Sorry to be nosy. It's just, I'm supposed to be on the lookout for, uh, you know, unusual stuff. For Attikol.
ME:	[Getting nervous.] Why would Attikol care?

And that's when I heard all about Attikol's fascination with the Magical World of Magic. Apparently he fancies himself quite the Mystical Dude, although he has absolutely no unusual talents aside from whatever a boatload of money can buy. He believes, get this, that many, many generations ago, his ancestors were robbed of their Great Mystical Power, and it is his DESTINY, handed down through a long line of rich jerks much like himself, to find and steal back the secret source of this power. Oh, my. I have to admit that did cheer me up quite a bit. Nothing like a belly laugh at someone else's expense to chase away the Amnesia Blues.

Then, of course, Jakey told me the sad part, which is that he hasn't seen his mother since he was a year old, because Attikol keeps him traveling from town to town, looking for that magical something.

ME: But what are you looking for, exactly?

J: Anything . . . unusual, I guess. Some kind of magical recipe in someone's mind, or whatever.

ME: [Feeling uncomfortable.] Are you going to tell him about my dress?

J: [Looking uncomfortable.] Um, well, I don't know, I mean, I probably SHOULD . . .

ME: [Feeling even more uncomfortable. Giving Jakey a "Don't Betray Your Only Friend" look.]

J: [Looking SUPER uncomfortable.] Uh, well, it's probably not what he's looking for, anyway. I guess.

ME: [Somewhat relieved.] Yeah, no point bugging him about a little old DRESS, right?

J: [Looking very relieved.] Yeah, no point talking to him about ANYTHING if I don't really have to.

Um, CREEPY!

I am feeling kind of afraid of Attikol right now.

Also, poor Jakey. Eight-ninths of his life on an adventure he doesn't want to be on. I mean, my adventure has only been twenty days long, and that's about twenty days too long for me.

Day 21

EXCELLENT RESEARCH TODAY.

OK. I FINALLY went upstairs to visit Schneider's grandma, the town vet. More on her later, but let me just say that she is INSANE!!! And get this, the entire attic of the El Dungeon is packed with Emma LeStrande's belongings, which used to be all set up in the Old Museum before the Mayor started holding slide shows and personal parties in there. And Mrs. Schneider, I mean Hilda, got all agitated when she saw me at her door, and even though I really couldn't understand a word she was saying, it was pretty obvious she wanted me to follow her up to the attic right away, which was pretty exciting in a kind of scarytale theater sort of way, like she was going to trap me in a giant birdcage, fatten me, and then eat me. So I followed her up there, and got to check out all that crazy lady's crazy stuff—crazy Emma, not crazy Hilda—but more on that later too. Right now I gotta tell you about this book. It was lying out on display on Emma's coffee table. It was a scrapbook of photos and news clippings going back decades. I sat down and started flipping through it and here is a list of the amazing things I have learned:

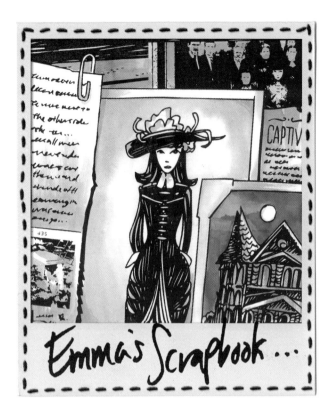

Emma's Scrapbook...

1. I look like Emma LeStrande!!!!!!!!!!!!!!!!!!!!!!!!!!!!!!!
2. I look a LOT like Emma LeStrande!!!!!!!!!!!!!!!!!!!!!!!
3. It is very unnerving, when you have amnesia and don't even know your own name, to keep encountering people who look just like you. Wonder if I could get a little break from the constant doppelgänger action?
4. Emma founded this town about seventy years ago with the idea that it would be a getaway spot for oddball

More from the scrapbook
of Emma LeStrande.

world travelers like herself. Her friends, in other words.

5. Back then, there were just two buildings in Blackrock:
   the El Dungeon and the bus depot.

6. About twenty years ago, this dude showed up, bought
   a plot of land from Emma, and built the junk-mail
   plant and City Hall, and called himself mayor. As
   they say, the rest is history.

7. As years went by and the mayor's friends moved in,

Emma sold everything except this building and the plot of land the minipark is on.

8. About 13 years ago, this building was actually wrapped in burlap, then drowned in plaster, and then painted beige. Thus its horrid shapelessness. No info on who did it, though evidence is pointing toward the mayor.

9. Found a photo of the El Dungeon before it was beige, and I REALLY think the beigeifying was a mistake. I mean, the building actually looked kind of good before that.

10. Geologists believe that biiiiiiillions of eons ago (give or take a year or so), there was an underground volcano here, and when it erupted, it made a huge crater, which over the ages developed into the bland dust bowl/dust serving tray we have here today. It also left behind some underground deposits of volcanic rock, and I'm guessing that's where Emma got the name for her town.

11. No relatives are mentioned in any of the clippings.

Emma's place, pre-beige.

12. I may or may not be related to Emma LeStrande, but either way I'm one of her people.
13. Emma LeStrande HAS to be a reason I'm here in Blackrock.

I WANT ACCESS TO MY MEMORIES. RIGHT NOW.

Well, my service request to the universe has been denied. Access to memories is being withheld. And yelling at the universe probably isn't going to get me what I want. And what I want is for a solution to rise up in front of me. Like the way I look at the espresso machine and just KNOW what it needs to hum along instead of croaking and wheezing.

You know what's crazy is that I looked at Raven last night and thought the exact same thing.

But that makes no sense at all and is probably evidence that I am losing my mind! So I'll just shut up about that now.

Anyway, back to Mrs. Schneider. I mean Hilda. She is elderly and foreign. Also, possibly loony. From what I could understand through her very brutal accent: No glue stuck like old Emma, the fleas are very ripe today, and hogs don't bark for nothing. I asked her if she'd stitched up any black cats' ears lately, and found out that the spiders of dawn are gumming up the turnstiles. (Which I took for a yes.)

So, no leads on the cats' owner, but I'm OK with that, because Emma's stuff in the attic was . . . it was SO GOOD. Granted,

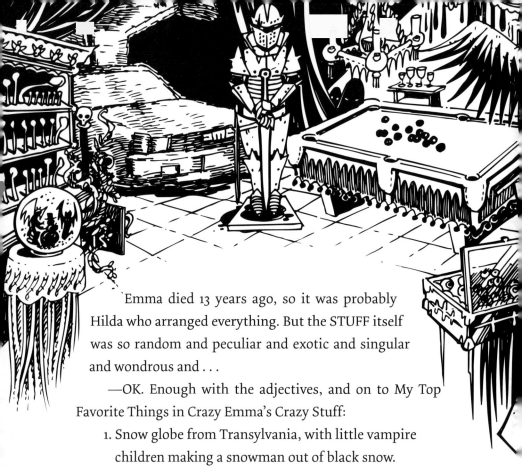

Emma died 13 years ago, so it was probably Hilda who arranged everything. But the STUFF itself was so random and peculiar and exotic and singular and wondrous and . . .

—OK. Enough with the adjectives, and on to My Top Favorite Things in Crazy Emma's Crazy Stuff:

1. Snow globe from Transylvania, with little vampire children making a snowman out of black snow.
2. Taxidermied vulture "eating" taxidermied bat.
3. Evil-looking Tiki god about the size of a hippopotamus.
4. Evil-looking doll with three-inch red fingernails—safely locked in glass case (whew!).
5. Really old bronze shield with an engraving of the town's imaginary black rock on it.
6. Decorative rack of really sharp, suspicious-looking souvenir grapefruit spoons.

7. Full set of knight's armor including battleaxe.

8. Ye Olde Mystery Object which is either a meteorite, the world's largest raisin, or a shrunken human head.

9. Box full of glass eyes, some human and some feline.

10. Pool table with fifteen 8-balls and nothing else.

11. A lifesize matchstick model of a DeLorean DMC-12.

12. Cyclopean fetal pig half-eaten by mites.

13. Antique crash-test dummy, made of . . . I don't know, porcelain? Yep, they don't make 'em like they used to!

Later

Curls is back at the café today. He was clearly surprised to see me. Turns out he has been spending less time milling about at the El Dungeon and more time milling about at the medicine show, trying to appear useful and get hired. He is refusing to accept the facts that

A) I am not Molly, and B) I am not qualified to give him advice on becoming more popular with Ümlaut's crew, no matter how much he begs. He was getting to be such a pest that I was forced to threaten him with slingshotting in sensitive areas of his anatomy. He retreated to a far table and has been sitting there glowering for the past two hours.

After getting him out of my hair, I was in a take-charge mood, and determined to get a straight story out of Raven for once, so I went and sat at the counter for about an hour asking her questions. GAHHHH BIRDBRAIN!! She would drive the Spanish Inquisition batty. Here is a tiny sample just to show the general flavor of my pain:

ME: So, where IS Rachel?
RAVEN: Uhhh, she's away.
ME: Where?
R: Iono.
ME: When is she coming back?
R: Iono.
ME: So who hired you?
R: Uhhh, the owner.
ME: So you've met Emma LeStrande?
R: Iono.
ME: Well, who pays you?
R: Huuuhhhhh?

ME: WHO SIGNS YOUR PAYCHECK? YOU GET PAID TO
     WORK HERE, RIGHT?

R: . . . . Iono?

So, yeah. After that, I kind of stopped wondering
what crimes Raven had committed and started
wondering who is taking care of Raven, instead.

Later

I walked around town with the cats for a while. I guess they'd
rather stick to the dark back alleys on our explorations, but I really
wanted to see what kind of progress Attikol had made on his challenge. Counted eleven buildings with full construction crews
working before I ran into Jakey—first time I've seen him outside
the psychic show or his own trailer. Makes sense. I can't stand people, either, and I don't have to hear their stupid thoughts. But a kid
has to buy parrot food sometimes.

I was kind of surprised that he had nothing to say about my
discoveries about Emma LeStrande. But I guess when you're a
nine-year-old boy, there are only a few things less boring than the
dead founders of towns. No matter how cool their collections
were.

He asked me if I knew any Egyptian jokes.

ME: No.

JAKEY: Oh yeah? Well, what did the one Egyptian say to

the other Egyptian when somebody farted?

ME: Don't know.

J: Ewwww, what sphinx? AHA HA HA HAHHAHA HAH AHHA!

ME: Yep.

J: What did the one Egyptian conjoined twin say to the other Egyptian conjoined twin?

ME: [Groaning in pain.][Long pause.] Well, go on.

J: We've got a lot of gut in common. AHA HA HA HA HA H HA HAH H AHHA H HA H H AH H HAH H AHHA!.....Get it?

ME: Yes. Yes, I get it.

J: Man, you should lose your memory more often.

ME: Oh. I see. I guess you've told me these before, huh?

J: [Laughing like maniac.] Hey, why did the Sphinx have to run to the bathroom?

After at least ten more jokes in that vein, I decided I would make the kid do me a favor in return for letting him torture me with terrible puns on "pyramid," "Cairo," and "sarcophagus." So I took him back to the El Dungeon to have him get a scope on Raven. Pointless—he couldn't read her at all! The only thing he could tell me was "She's not like other people." Duh+Duh=DUH.

Had him do a quick walk-through of the other customers' minds just in case. Here are the pathetic results:

1. Curls thinks Ümlaut and his crew have really improved the El Dungeon by breaking and replacing all its old furniture.
2. Curls still doesn't believe I'm not Molly. Delusional!
3. Curls DOES (finally) believe I have amnesia. Since it explains why I don't hang out with him.
4. Curls is peeved that I have been ignoring him and hanging out with Jakey. (!!!)
5. Curls has a crush on Raven.
6. HamHawk has a crush on Raven.
7. Ditto Hurk, Steve, and Grapey.
8. Hurk thinks Ümlaut's Pätented Pötion of Pöwer is going to cure his male-pattern baldness.
9. Steve thinks Ümlaut's Pätented Pötion of Pöwer is going to help him win the lottery.
10. Grapey thinks the Pätented Pötion is a bunch of hööëy, but bought a crate of bottles for ironic presents to hipster friends in big cities.
11. HamHawk really misses Sizzle and Petal, who sold their house to Attikol and bailed town two days ago.
12. Every customer including HamHawk has plans to sell Attikol their homes at inflated prices and leave Blackrock in the next few days.
13. Every customer has a triumphant, rebellious, embarrassing Goodbye and Eat My Dust speech prepared for their manager at the junk-mail factory.

Gahh! I feel sorrier than ever for Jakey!! Also, a little creeped out. I mean, I don't have anything to hide, but if/when I get rid of the amnesia, I don't want him reading MY mind.

Later

Since I got back I've been noticing that Raven has been having trouble talking. I mean, even for her. She has a bad case of the hiccups, which has gone on for the past day or so. Today she made me a sandwich, but it was inside-out. And she's been doing a lot of chewing stare, without the chewing. I keep thinking I see spiders crawling out of her neck, but it's only her hair. All around I would say she's looking pretty poorly. If she were an espresso machine I'd say she's in dire need of a tune-up.

Day 22

What a depressing day.

First, I decided it was time to see if my dress is really as special as Sharon thought. Turns out it is. It doesn't seem there are any limits to what it can hold. I put all of the following in the pockets and there's not even a bulge:

1. 16 Blackrock newspapers
2. 13 soda cans with spiders in them
3. 3 French toast
4. 1 Polaroid camera
5. 37 slingshotting rocks

6. 1 slingshot

7. 7 pieces of scrap lumber from the Dumpster

8. 11 (empty) espresso cups

9. HamHawk's chessboard

10. Raven's cape

11. 2 shoes

12. 1 metric grip of junk mail

13. 4 black cats

I should be excited about this, but knowing what I know about Attikol, I find it very worrisome. I mean, the dress is obviously more than just special. In fact, I'll go ahead and say I think it's downright unusual.

It was all starting to make me feel more and more uncomfortable about seeing Jakey again, because it was looking more and more like something he really should tell Attikol about, if he ever wants to see his home and family again. And really, why should I expect him not to tell? I have nothing to offer him. I don't mind hanging out with him for now; it's been fun playing video games and gossiping with him—but once the amnesia's gone, I'll be like everyone else: avoiding him to protect my privacy.

And it doesn't matter how rotten I feel about that. I'm not Molly Merriweather. I can only stand so much human contact.

On the other hand, I am reeeeeeeally nervous about what Attikol might do if he finds out my dress is so . . . unusual.

Later

Just my luck—while I was thinking over all of this, Jakey showed up at the El D. Talk about awkward.

I kind of wish he wouldn't leave his trailer. I guess he's lonely, but hearing all those random people's thoughts makes him awfully testy. And more selfishly, I would rather be the one to decide when I'm gonna share the contents of my brain with the Moon Child. You know?

Anyway. What made it all even more than awkward was what Jakey had to say, and this is pretty embarrassing to write: He asked me if I would want to join the medicine show. Said they were looking for a crystal-ball reader. Said he had some ideas on how to turn my "special" dress into some kind of magic act, and how we wouldn't even need to explain it to Attikol. Said I could bring the cats, as long as they didn't bug his parrot. Said he could really handle having a friend, especially one with a bad case of amnesia.

Unfortunately for Jakey, he knew my answer as soon as I did.

Later

As if the day wasn't bad enough already!

Raven made the same cappuccino order over 100 times while HamHawk and I tried to figure out how to stop her. She is extremely strong. I would even say she has the strength of five men. I say this because HamHawk, who has the weight of five men, had to sit on her to finally get her to stop.

I told all the customers we were closed and now I'm sitting here wondering what in fog's name I'm going to do. Maybe Raven needs a doctor? A vet? Some quality secret closet time??

Man, this blows.

Later

GOOD STUFF!!!!

I was sitting at the counter staring at Raven, trying to get her to talk and pondering what I would even tell a doctor if I took her to one. "Uh, the problem is, she was making all this espresso . . . and wouldn't stop . . . making espresso. Do you have a pill for that?" Right. But the more I stared at her, the more I was convinced she didn't need a doctor any more than a broken cash register would need a doctor. I stared and stared and stared at her and then I saw the clasp behind her ear. Reached over and released it, swung her ear right off her head like a little door. And then her controls were there under it and I could check the calibrations and such.

Crazy, huh?

She's well-made, that Raven. Great craftsmanship. But definitely the type of

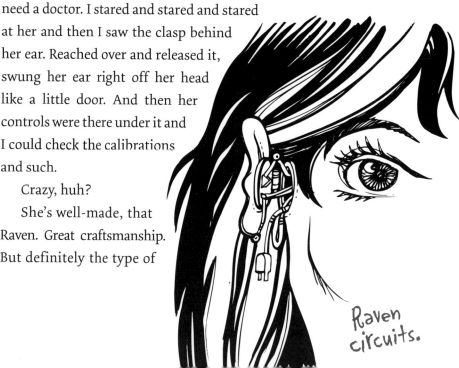

Raven circuits.

machine (android? robot? golem?) that needs regular maintenance. Otherwise, inside-out sandwiches and endless espresso, apparently. While I was in there tuning things up, I noticed that she'd been dialed way down—no wonder I thought she was such a birdbrain! She was so grateful when I got her back up to some smarter operating. Sandwiches are back to normal, no more hiccups, AND she can speak in complete sentences. Still not much of a conversationalist, though. And still short on useful information.

ME: So, Raven, who hired you to work here?

RAVEN: The owner.

ME: Do you know who the owner is?

R: I'm programmed not to answer that question.

ME: Wow. Well, do you know who I am?

R: You're my assistant. Earwig.

ME: Do you know who made you?

R: I'm programmed not to answer that question.

ME: Of course you are. Do you know where Rachel is?

R: She went away.

ME: But you didn't hurt her?

R: No.

Would LOVE to find out who made her. (Emma LeStrande???) And what she's programmed to do, besides make coffee and sandwiches and give evasive answers to crucial questions.

And why she showed up here the same time I did.

Later

I just realized that, of course, Raven is . . . unusual, meaning Attikol might be interested in her for more than just loooove.

I guess I can add that to the growing list of things I don't want Jakey to know about.

Really late the same day (I think)

Higgined! I should have checked out Raven's secret closet a looooooooong time ago.

The first part you see when you go in is no big deal. A tiny little room with a mirror on the wall, a little shelf, a bag of cosmetics with RACHEL written on it. Emergency rations of water and astronaut food. Some coat hooks on the wall. Your basic extremely tiny, suspiciously secret employee break room, I guess.

BUT.

As soon as I went in I felt different. Recharged or espressofied. And like my eyes were sharper, or something. All the little fibers in the shag carpeting stood out so clearly. So right away I noticed the small ridges in the carpet that outlined the trapdoor underneath.

The cats and I have spent a good long time in there. Down there. It goes way, way, way down. Farther than you'd ever think.

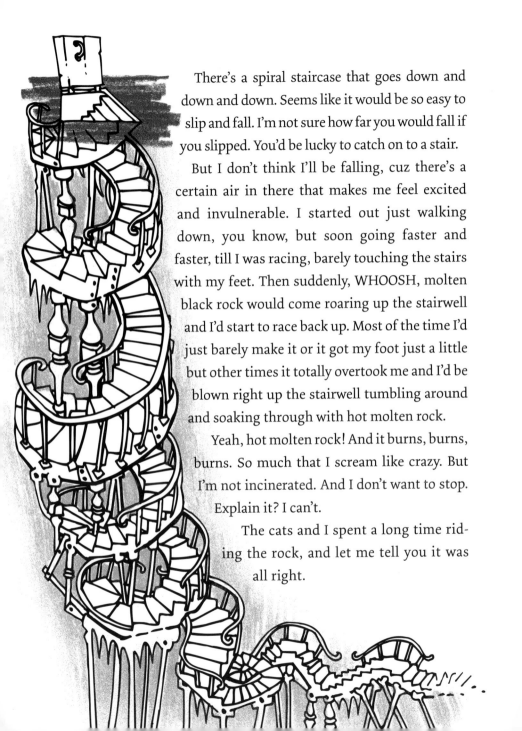

There's a spiral staircase that goes down and down and down. Seems like it would be so easy to slip and fall. I'm not sure how far you would fall if you slipped. You'd be lucky to catch on to a stair.

But I don't think I'll be falling, cuz there's a certain air in there that makes me feel excited and invulnerable. I started out just walking down, you know, but soon going faster and faster, till I was racing, barely touching the stairs with my feet. Then suddenly, WHOOSH, molten black rock would come roaring up the stairwell and I'd start to race back up. Most of the time I'd just barely make it or it got my foot just a little but other times it totally overtook me and I'd be blown right up the stairwell tumbling around and soaking through with hot molten rock.

Yeah, hot molten rock! And it burns, burns, burns. So much that I scream like crazy. But I'm not incinerated. And I don't want to stop. Explain it? I can't.

The cats and I spent a long time riding the rock, and let me tell you it was all right.

Next day (I think)—Day . . . 23?
(Haven't slept. Losing track of time.)

I reeeeeeallly wish I'd checked out the closet better back when I first discovered it. But I didn't know then that Raven herself was so . . . unusual.

Today I went down the staircase a lot more slowly and detective-like. There are all these landings that are sort of protected from the black rock when it whooshes. Here's a short list of stuff I found:

1. A bookcase of fascinating titles like <u>Occult Thermodynamics and You</u>.
2. A door locked with three complicated bolts.
3. A loose brick that reveals a secret cubbyhole full of the most darling bright red spiders.
4. A bunch of hidey-holes you can use to stay dryish when the lava whooshes up.
5. A large oil painting of a menacing black rock.
6. A folder full of architectural sketches for the attractive black building that the El Dungeon once was.
7. A telephone nook with one of those old-timey black phones, the kind with a dial and a cord (not working).
8. A beaten-up tin box full of miscellaneous electrical parts.
9. A bucket on a pulley.
10. A coat hook with a lab coat hanging on it (nothing in pockets).

11. A wooden bench covered in carved graffiti—must do rubbings of it later.

12. Some extremely pleasing rocks for slingshotting.

13. 4 giant statues of cats done in hard, glassy black rock.

Later—possibly a lot later (??)

Have pulled up and let down the bucket many, many times, but there is never anything in the bucket except hot liquid black rock.

Later

I JUST realized I haven't slept at all or eaten anything since I first went down into the closet. I wonder why? I'm not hungry or sleepy, and I feel incredible. Like I could fly. There must be something about this place that's recharging me.

Uh-oh.

Doesn't that pretty much point to the black rock being . . . unusual?

And therefore, something that Attikol would like to get his hands on?

Am feeling the need for big-time diversionary self-preservationist tactics.

It's all making me feel extremely lost and alone. It wouldn't be so bad if I could at least remember some of the good advice I'm sure my mom has given me over the years. I've been trying to prompt my memory by saying out loud: "It's like Mom always said . . ." But I get nothing.

4 black cats sniffing 4 black cat statues.

Am holding tight to that folded piece of paper I found in my pocket, the one I instructed myself not to open until Day 27. I reeeeeeally hope it contains some kind of lifeline, such as my mom's phone number, or a recipe for reversing amnesia.

Hope I can hold out a few more days on my own before I give in and open it.

Day 24

You know what I've realized today? It is VERY suspicious that Schneider never told me I looked like the dead founder of his town. And I KNOW he's seen Emma LeStrande's portrait. I mean, I did think it was kind of odd, but excusable, that he'd never looked through the scrapbook with all those photos of her. But I started to suspect him today when I took Sabbath to Hilda's to get his stitches taken out, and I saw a photo of Hilda and Emma and a teenaged Schneider on Hilda's mantelpiece. Even THAT was KIND of excusable because . . . well, MAYBE he had forgotten what Emma looked like in the 13 years since she had died. (AND hadn't visited his grandma in all that time.) But THEN I went inside CITY HALL for the first time to find Schneider, and there is a six-foot by ten-foot portrait of Emma hanging in the foyer!!! I was so shocked I turned right around and came back to the El Dungeon to think it over. He is clearly hiding things from me!! But WHY??? Would dearly love to get a sneak peek into his mind. Wish I could ask Jakey to take a look for me, but I have to steer clear of the Moon Child unless I want Attikol to know about Raven and her secret closet full of magical black rock.

Oh Duh. Jakey can't hear Raven's thoughts. (That, or Raven doesn't HAVE thoughts. Whatever.)

I just hope she can follow instructions.

Later

I sent Raven out to Jakey's trailer with the following note:

> Yo Jakey,
>
> Sorry I haven't been to see you in a while but am very sick with laryngitis. Anyway, how would you like to do me a favor? I will owe you big-time. There's this dude Schneider who hangs out at City Hall who knows all kinds of stuff about me that he won't tell. Maybe you can get something interesting out of him. I told Raven to buy you some parrot toys if you want.
>
> ~~Later~~ Your Friend,
> Earwig

Now I'm making espresso for the regulars while Raven does my dirty work for me. Am crossing my fingers that all goes well.

Three Hours Later

MUCH PROGRESS! Raven is back! She had a letter for me from Jakey, which I'm pasting on the next page.

Hi Earwig,

Sory you are sick. I would come see you but Attikol will have a fit if I get larginitus. Sorry for ~~terribel~~ terrible spelling Anyway the wierdest thing happened when Raven came here! She and my parrot were totally talking! I mean in bird language not English. I told you she is not like other poeple! Man she is the wierdest person I ever met eccept for you.

Anyway she took me down to city hall and we found Shenider. Yah he has a lot of ideas about you. First off he thinks you are related to this dead ~~frend~~ fiend of his name Emma. And did you know there is this giant picture of you on the wall there. And he thinks you are smarter than him and you will figure him out and be relly mad that he made you go to school and you will tell Emma on him wich seems kind of dum since she is dead and all. And he has a letter from Emma about you that I copied down for you.

That's pretty much it about you. he also is trying to figure out how to stop Attikol from recking all these buildings in town. so maybe we will be leaving town soon Also Raven took me to the pet store and bought me a bunch of parrot toys and so its relly ok that she is so wierd! Also a lot of buildings are looking relly bad like they might fall down. HAHAHA. I hope Attikol gets in trouble for it.

> Bye,
> Jakey

And here is the letter from Emma that Jakey apparently pulled out of Schneider's mind.

My dear Mr. Schneider,

As I am writing this, you are thirteen years old; but when you receive it, you will be twenty-six, and I will be long dead. I am arranging with a friend to deliver this at the proper time. When that time comes, a certain great-niece of mine will be arriving in Blackrock with the intention of accomplishing several tasks for me. I suspect that you will have no trouble recognizing her.

I am enclosing a sum of money that you may use to secure yourself a position on the City Council. (I am sure that things will have changed considerably in Blackrock in thirteen years— yet somehow I feel just as sure that the corruption and graft brought in by our Mayor will not have changed one whit. I do wish I had the strength to run him out, but I am old—you have no idea how old—and very, very tired.) In return, I ask that you use your position to assist my great-niece if she should need your aid.

A word of caution. You may assume that she is just as capable and intelligent as you are (if not more so), but she may be operating under certain…shall we say, self-imposed handicaps. Therefore, I am requesting that you interfere with her as little as possible, but provide whatever help she asks of you.

Thank you in advance for your kind assistance. I hope to receive an excellent report of your conduct from my great-niece. You may expect a fitting reward—"from beyond the grave," as you young people say!

Yours, Emma LeStrande

Am in shock.

Am really in shock.

Also, am REALLY hoping the bird-talk episode wasn't anything Jakey feels he should mention to Attikol. Also, did not realize Jakey's psychic power was so burly that he can pull entire letters out of people's minds!! Also, couldn't Schneider have been a LITTLE more helpful?? Also, have clearly used my quota of capital letters and exclamation points for today, but CRABBING GOLDFRIX!!!!!!!!!! I wish Old Emma (Great-Aunt Emma?) had sent ME a nice explanatory letter!

Well hey now. Who's to say she didn't? Maybe I just haven't found it yet.

OK.

Here's what I ~~know~~ HOPE I know:

1. If I can believe the above letter, then I'm the great-niece of Emma LeStrande.

2. I was probably correct in guessing that I'm here in Blackrock to accomplish something, and that something is linked to Great-Aunt Emma.

3. Great-Aunt Emma seemed to know a lot about things that would be going down 13 years after she died.

4. There's a possibility I can communicate with Great-Aunt Emma, if I can only figure out how.

5. Based on Jakey's note, he doesn't seem to recognize that telling the future and communicating from beyond the

grave are highly . . . unusual talents. Am feeling glad that he is only nine, and all he knows of the world is the medicine show and the weirdos who run it. Fingers crossed that I'm correct here.

6. Schneider seems to think Great-Aunt Emma will be pissed to find out that he forced me to go to school.

7. I kind of wish I COULD get Schneider in trouble, but at least I know I have something to threaten him with.

8. Schneider is a shameless double-crosser and lives in a world of lies, BUT, he did tell me to check out the library's collection of Emma LeStrande stuff back on Day 11, so I guess I can just torment him a little, rather than destroying him utterly.

9. I really do need to visit the library's collection of Emma LeStrande stuff.

10. I also should be spending more quality time with my great-aunt's belongings.

11. The secret closet and the liquid black rock are linked to some . . . unusual side effects. Possibly more unusual than not needing to eat or sleep. In other words: I can expect pretty much ANYTHING from Great-Aunt Emma.

12. I am going to search that secret closet for evidence that Great-Aunt Emma made Raven.

13. Great-Aunt Emma expected that I would be very smart. I need to live up to that. For my own sake.

Well what do you know? I found a book down in Closet Land called <u>Secrets of Golem Dominion</u>. It does not tell you how to make a golem, and seeing as how it was written about a hundred years ago, I wouldn't expect it to say much about a golem like Raven, who is running some pretty complicated technology. BUT. Here is the cool part, which I'm copying from page 23:

"Having completed the rites to animate the golem, you must place it under your command, and once this is accomplished, you may be assured, there is no power on earth that may divert your golem from carrying out your decrees, nor will the mandates of any other person have effect."

Isn't that interesting, I said to myself as I read this, thinking about how I sent Raven out on errands with the Moon Child.

So.

I asked Raven to come out to the back alley with me. Told her to stand on one leg, hop up and down, bark like a dog, and rip a steel panel off the Dumpster.

All of which she immediately did.

Just to test things, I went back inside and asked HamHawk to come try giving her some commands.

All that happened was that they both looked at me really funny.

AHAHAHAHHAHAHAHAH I MADE A GOLEM
I MADE A GOLEM AHAHAHHAHAHAHAHAHAH

I HAVE A GOLEM WHO FOLLOWS MY EVERY COMMAND AHAHAHAHHAHAHAHAH

—OK.

No point in getting too cocky.

After all, I don't know how smart I'm really proving myself to be. Lots of leads, very few answers. Nearly thirty days of failure. And you might think it would make me feel better to know that I'm capable of making, programming, and repairing a golem . . . but in some way Raven is now the hardest person in this whole place for me to be around. Because every time I look at her, I'm reminded that once upon a time, I was smart. Smart enough to make a person out of . . . whatever I made her out of. I mean, I'm not saying she's perfect. She may not be great at conversation. Not that I would want her to be. And she really can only make espresso and sandwiches. Although, when it comes down to it, I wouldn't want to eat much else.

Hmm . . .

Maybe these are not design flaws.

Maybe I should do a little more investigation on what she can and can't do.

Later

Am feeling smarter. Here's why.

RAVEN CAN'T ...	BUT RAVEN CAN ...
Hold a scintillating conversation	Talk to birds
Make pork chops, roast chicken, filet mignon, etc.	Make a killer cheese and avocado sandwich
Tell me what 10 divided by 2 is	Tell me how much 3 double lattes and 2 americanos would be, with tax
Do a somersault	Rip apart a steel Dumpster
Ride a bike	Drive a car . . . or a VAN

Do you SEE that last item?? THAT is why she and I are headed to City Hall to meet Schneider as soon as they're open.

Day 25

Things are looking up!!!!!

It's surprising what people will do for you if they think you are smarter than they are. Also, if they feel guilty because of something bad that happened to you. Also, if they think you'll get them in trouble with a dead lady. Anyway, I didn't even tell Schneider about my new information—and still, he was like putty in my hands. PUTTY! Within twenty minutes he was telling the officer at the auto impound lot that the van was Raven's, and it only SEEMED like the license plate wasn't registered because Blackrock doesn't subscribe to the National Registry of Highly Unusual Automobiles, which he clearly just made up, and that he was sure $20 would cover the ticket, the towing, AND the month in the impound . . . Well, it looked like a Jedi mind trick to me, but maybe the guy just owed him a favor. Whatever! The van is ours! Schneider is OK in my book!

And Oh My Frog, that's not even the good part. The good part was when the four of us went out to the van and the officer cut off the chains and handed Raven the key, and she opened the driver's door and got in like she totally knew what she was doing, and then reached down into her cleavage, and took out her driver's license and the title of the van, which is in her name.

!!!

(Her last name, in case you were wondering, because I sure was, is not Dungeon, but Miller. Ha! Ha!)

AND, the GREAT part is that OUR marvelous van is now parked in the alley behind the El Dungeon where the lean-to used to be.

I gave Fridge Box II

a decent burial in the Dumpster out back. But I wasn't all that sad to see it go.

Oh. AND. The WONDERFUL part. The splendorous, beautimous, fantastiffical part is this: If the cats belong with the van, and the van belongs to my golem, and my golem belongs to me, then all of that adds up to one thing:

the Cats are Mine!!!

Had a knockdown, laughing, meowing, squirming hugfest with them to celebrate.

Later

Have found the

Letter From Emma!!!!!!!!!

Here's how it happened: I was
hanging out in the van trying to
have a nice, relaxing nightmare,
or get some inspiration for
my next breakthrough,
or, I don't know,
fully recover
from amnesia, and ~~the~~ my cats were being just extremely pesky.
Instead of piling on top of me as instructed, they were all over the
van, walking on my face, making their collars jingle in my ear,
tussling one another, etc.—at least, Miles, NeeChee, and Sabbath
were doing all that. When I sat up to open the door and let them
out, I saw that McFreely was quietly scratching up the upholstery
from the floor between the two front seats. Now . . . I just don't know
what to think of this. Maybe it's all a coincidence, but I think it's
fairly odd that she would A) Get the boy cats distracting me, B)
Scratch RIGHT THERE, of all places, C) Stop when she had pulled up
enough of the upholstery to reveal the corner of the letter, and D)
Look directly at me and meow like "Are you happy?"

She is a very mysterious feline!!

Anyway, the Letter's on the next page.

171

My dear great-niece,

How unfortunate it is that you and I will never meet, but fate has ordained that I will be dead before you are born. I am arranging with a friend to have this letter delivered to you once you are thirteen years of age. Understand, as I do, that knowing each other in life is hardly necessary; you and I will grow to know each other quite well nonetheless. As a sort of introduction, I am leaving you all of my property, and ask that you lay claim to it as soon as possible. Of course you will need to prove yourself worthy first.

The situation is as follows. Your inheritance, including one asset in particular of exceptional value, rests in a small town called Blackrock. I am enclosing a sum of money so that you can make the necessary plans to spend some time away from home. I leave the decision in your hands, but I suspect you will want to devise a subterfuge so that no parent or guardian insists on accompanying you.

I give you this stern warning: A very serious threat currently exists in Blackrock—a person who, if the facts were revealed, would stop at *nothing* to rob you of what is rightfully yours. Do not, under any circumstance, approach Blackrock until your defenses are prepared. At the very least, you will need to be incognito. If only there were some way you could defend your very *mind*—but I am afraid that is impossible, or that the solution is beyond my tired old brain. Dear niece, I would like to say that I have every confidence that you will find a way to remove the threat and take full possession of your property. My sources have assured me that you have a better chance of success than most people would. However, I must be honest with you: Your opponent is powerful and has even more powerful allies.

I apologize for the dearth of solid information in this letter, but I am sure you understand that it is impossible. This letter is incriminating enough already, and if it should fall into the wrong hands . . . One thing I can give you: a point of contact—my employee, Rachel, at a café called the El Dungeon. It will be a good place for you to start.

Follow your dreams, my child.

Your great-aunt,

Emma LeStrange

Whew.

Where do I begin with all that?

Well, I'm going to make the following ~~educated~~ wild guesses:

1. My goal here in Blackrock is to take possession of my inheritance—Great-Aunt Emma's estate.

2. The estate probably consists of the El Dungeon building and all its oddball treasures, the amazing secret closet, and, uh, the minipark, or something.

3. The one exceptionally valuable asset is probably either, I don't know, the matchstick DeLorean (ha), or the customer base at the El Dump (ahahahah). Seriously though, I bet the real treasure is hidden behind the locked door in the secret closet.

4. Possible opponents: the mayor? The police—nah, she said "powerful"! Attikol? Ümlaut? Curls? Crazy Hilda??? Would like to think it's the police, or Curls . . . but am afraid it is probably Attikol.

5. It seems that, at least for now, my opponent doesn't realize he's my opponent: He hasn't discovered that my inheritance is valuable to him.

6. Great-Aunt Emma expected there would be some kind of attack on my mind. Which I am afraid is probably Jakey's psychic power.

7. In light of current information, I now have a much better attitude toward my bad case of amnesia. Still, I will have

to be extremely careful to prevent Jakey from knowing about certain . . . unusual items.

8. I could just wait for Professor Ümlaut's Prophylactery and Revue and Uncle Attikol's Deadly Dollhouse to leave town, and then claim my inheritance, except

    8A) They come here every year, and

    8B) Because of the stupid challenge I gave Attikol, he now owns most of Blackrock.

9. So I guess I have to somehow get Attikol (and Jakey) to leave Blackrock forever. Without letting them know why.

10. Even if I do manage to accomplish this, I still don't know how I'm going to get my memory back.

11. Rachel totally bailed on her duty to help me out. Where is she, anyway? And why isn't she here, helping me out?

12. Whatever subterfuge I devised to keep my parent or guardian from accompanying me to Blackrock, it's bound to have some kind of time limit. Which could be either my salvation or my complete undoing.

13. I am screwed.

Day 26

HamHawk made his emotional goodbyes to Raven today. He has sold his house to Attikol like everyone else and is moving to Chicago. I have been too wrapped up in closet-diving, van-reclaiming, and mystery-solving to think about it, but now I realize I haven't seen any of the other regulars in at least a full day. Curls and the Ümlaut crew are still here as usual, but they've lost some of their steam now that they have no audience but themselves. Anyway, it was hurting me to watch HamHawk tell Raven wistful things like "I'll call you from Chicago, OK?" when she was barely responding, so I went out to walk around town and scope the situation a bit. The streets of Blackrock are looking surprisingly empty, aside from unwanted belongings being piled up on the sidewalk as people leave town. Many, many buildings are also empty. Most of them have been pushed one inch to the east and are now in the process of falling down. And almost all the rest have construction crews working to push them one inch to the east. Thereby knocking them down. I guess buildings don't take well to being pushed to the east. Lucky for Attikol I never specified they had to stay intact.

Had a moment of terror when I remembered my dream about black liquid coming up from under all those buildings. But everything is looking safely dry. Well, that's one good thing to hold on to. And all these other things still to worry me: Great-Aunt Emma is still technically the owner of the El Dungeon. And she's dead. What is going to happen if/when Attikol tries to buy it? If Emma didn't leave a will, could I claim ownership just because, um, I look a lot like her? And let's imagine I did own the building. How far would Attikol go to complete his challenge? If the worst happens, and Attikol somehow does push the El Dungeon to the east, how am I going to keep him away from Raven?

What if Jakey comes to see whether I'm over the laryngitis?
What if I accidentally see Jakey on the street?

Later

While thinking this, I suddenly got very nervous and ducked into the nearest building, which happened to be the library. So I figured it was high time I saw the Emma LeStrande room. Hogbark! That was some good stuff. There is another large portrait of Great-Aunt Emma there. With her looking over me, I started reading through the documents she left. (Of course I was hoping for a will, but no dice.) They were all copies of patent applications—you know, those things you turn in to the government when you invent something, so that no one can steal your idea. Here are my favorites:

1. Mechanical linen-blackener
2. Amplitudinal sandstorm generator
3. Snake kibble
4. Leafblower annihilator
5. Automatic irrigation and feeding system for carnivorous plants
6. Cat thoughtwave amplifier
7. Method for bronzing live animals without hurting them
8. Organic electric wiring to be used inside living plants
9. Unbreakable polymer filament synthesized from coffee grounds
10. Earwig trap (laughed my cheeks off at that one)

Dude, I think I love my dead Great-Aunt Emma.

11. Magnetic paint
12. Method for spinning cat hair into yarn
13. Hotrodded slingshot with hidden compartments

Later

Ran into Schneider on my way back from the library, which was kind of convenient, since he is the only person I could think of who might be able to answer some of my current questions. I decided to lay it all out for him.

ME: Look, Schneider, I know everything.

SCHNEIDER: Wow, you got your memory back?

ME: Uh . . . no. I mean . . . I know all about that letter you got from my great-aunt Emma.

S: . . . How could you possibly know that?

ME: Uh, Great-Aunt Emma told me. From beyond the grave?

S: Oh.

ME: I was wondering about the reward she promised you. Because . . . she . . . said I should find out what you want.

S: Well, uh, I don't know if I actually deserve any reward. But, yeah, when you talk to her again, let her know, there is something, I mean, I don't know if she could do it, maybe it's not even worth asking, but . . .

ME: Spit it out, Schneider.

S: [Blushing like crazy.] I want to be mayor of Blackrock.

ME: [Laughing like crazy.] No problem, dude. I will definitely tell her.

Man, who knew Schneider was so mental?—Anyhoodle, what's important is that he also coughed up the following information:

1. He confirmed that he owes Great-Aunt Emma a favor because she gave him enough money to pay a huge bribe and get elected to City Council.

2. Come to find out, Schneider is also Head of the Sanitation Department, Fire Marshal, and Coordinator of Charitable Activities. (Like I said—Mental!)

3. As far as he knows, EVERYONE has sold their property to Attikol, including himself, excluding my dead Great-Aunt Emma, who could not be persuaded to sell, being dead.

4. Schneider did not want to sell, but the price kept going

higher and higher, and then there was some mention of kneecapping, so he thought it best to agree.

5. He's now staying in Hilda's spare room upstairs from the El Dungeon.

6. He knows that Attikol has been looking for Great-Aunt Emma's will. So has Schneider. Nothing so far.

7. It would be pretty easy for Schneider to transfer ownership of her properties to me if we act fast, before all the town officials leave for good.

8. He says it is common knowledge that Attikol A) prides himself on never, never losing a challenge, and B) has never, never been so smitten with a lady as he is with Raven.

9. Rumor has it that the Mayor accepted a pretty staggering sum of money to give Attikol permission to go ahead and push the El Dungeon to the east once everyone is gone.

10. Schneider hopes I have some clever ideas on preventing this, since he doesn't think Attikol will let a little thing like ownership stand in his way.

11. Schneider recommends that I do like him and pack my belongings in preparation for fleeing town, since he is sure the El Dungeon will be rubble in a day or two.

12. Schneider is being a major Mr. Bring-Down right now.

13. Schneider really DOES believe I can communicate with Great-Aunt Emma. He said I should say "hi" and "sorry" for him. Wow.

Day 27

Have done something very, very shameful.

Was feeling super-overwhelmed after yesterday's conversation with Schneider. No idea how I am supposed to deal with all this stuff about Emma's will and fighting Attikol for her property. Was getting very weak-hearted with thoughts like "I'm just a kid" and "The SMART thing to do here is . . . to panic" and so, I'm sorry to report, I took out the folded bit of paper that I found in my pocket on Day 20, and opened it up.

Was extremely excited to see "MOM" and a phone number. Blessed Mom. Blessed emergency hotline to Mom.

I hunkered down behind the counter of the El Dungeon and dialed.

SOMEONE: Hello?

ME: [Hm, doesn't sound like a mom voice. Do I have a sister?] Mom? Is Mom there?

S: Hello? Oh . . . Earwig!

ME: [Good grog, is my name actually Earwig?] Hi! Can I talk to Mom?

S: Dude, Earwig, it's me, Molly.

ME: Oh . . . . Molly. Wow. Uh, sorry, I was actually trying to get in touch with my mom.

MOLLY: Oh, well, I'm not staying there anymore, actually. Right now I'm in this crazy town called Zip Down, Pennsylvania.

ME: Wait, so . . . [Molly was staying with MY mom? No. No. Brain will not process.]

M: You sound kinda out of it. Did you give yourself another case of amnesia, or what?

ME: Uh, something like that. Um, so, uh, have we met?

M: You bet we've met! Hey, listen. You don't need to say any more. I know you wouldn't have called unless you needed help, so just hang in there and I'll be in Blackrock as soon as I can!

ME: Wait . . . you don't need to come . . .

M: Yeah, it'll be so jelly! Tell Ripper I'm coming. Maybe he and I can pick our next town together.

ME: Seriously, all I need is my mom's number.

M: Well, unfortunately I don't have it. Look, we'll figure out your mystery together! It'll be sooooooo peakin'!

And she said goodbye.

Man, I do not want Molly here!

Especially not if she thinks she is going to solve any mystery with ME. Or that it'll be at all "peakin'."

Not much I can do about it, except . . . solve everything before she gets here.

GASP! OF!! HORROR!!!!!

What was that Molly said?

"Did you give yourself another case of amnesia, or what?"

No no no please don't tell me I did this to MYSELF?????

What am I . . . evil?

please please let her be wrong please let me not be that diabolical I don't want to be the one keeping myself in total amnesia I don't think I can take it anymore and there's nothing I can do I've trapped myself here and how can I outsmart myself?

Later

Jeez. Have been sitting here considering whether I should tear out the above entry out of sheer embarrassment. Have calmed down and reconsidered the situation, which is looking more and more interesting, and . . . well, more and more hopeful. Really, I should have realized all this when I first read Great-Aunt Emma's letter. OF COURSE I did this to myself, to protect myself, as instructed by Great-Aunt Emma. And this is good news. If I created the amnesia, then surely (SURELY?) I had some kind of plan to reverse it.

Broggling harmwarts, let's hope so.

Later

Capable of making a golem. Capable of inflicting amnesia on myself, not once but twice. NOT capable of figuring out how to keep the El Dungeon from getting knocked down.

OK. At a loss. No clue what to do. No one to ask, except . . .

Nah. No way. Never going to happen.

Oh, what the hey.

Um, hello, Great-Aunt Emma?

You there?

I need to ask for some help.

I could really use a clue on how to get Attikol out of town.

Nothing, huh? Not much of a talker? That's cool.

Tell you what, since I don't have a ouija board, we can use my notebook. I'll shake it and then open it to a random page. You just guide me to a page that has a clue for me. And I'll try to figure it out. Sound good?

OK here we go.

OK, Day 26, yesterday. OK, let's see what we got. HamHawk left. And I went to the library. Saw all your patent applications. Talked to Schneider about you. OK, not sure what the clue is. Let's try that again.

OK, Day 26. Yep. Well, Schneider is looking for your will. That's probably part of the solution, right? Let's try again just to be safe.

Wow, Day 26 again. OK, there is definitely something there I need to figure out.

OK, Great-Aunt Emma, I'm gonna work on that. Oh, and . . . this is kinda embarrassing, but Schneider says hi, and he wants to be mayor of Blackrock.

Later

Strange things are afoot at the El D!! Am very grateful for Raven, Great-Aunt Emma, and the fact that golems and ghosts get along like . . . two preternatural things that get along really well, instead of trying to destroy each other, or at least gnaw on each other's souls, like preternatural things normally do. Wait, do preternatural things even have souls? —Anyway.

I had been sitting around asking Raven random questions and trying to free up my mind on what my next move should be.

ME:	Hey, Raven, are you really a raven?
Raven:	Maybe. Sort of. Iono.
ME:	Do the cats want to eat you?
R:	Hope not.
Me:	Did I make you out of dead people?
R:	Hope not.
ME:	How old are you?
R	23. I mean, 3. I mean, 93. Iono.
ME:	Are you going to live a long time?

R: Iono.

ME: Talked to any birds lately?

R: No birds here.

ME: What did Jakey's parrot tell you?

R: She has lice.

ME: How am I gonna stop Attikol from knocking down the El Dungeon?

R: Uhhhhhhh . . .

ME: I mean, I'm not asking for the whole grand plan . . . Just a little something. A diversion would be nice, to start with.

R: Sandstorm.

ME: WHAT DID YOU SAY?

R: [Flickers of superior intelligence in her face . . . I swear.] Sandstorm.

ME: [Heart beating hard.] How did you get that idea?

R: Iono.

ME: [Getting very excited.] Where is Great-Aunt Emma's will?

R: There is no will, my dear.

ME: AUNT EMMA, IS THAT YOU?

R: . . . . . . Huhhhhh?

ME: Great-Aunt Emma, did you make a will?

R: What's a will?

Me: GAH . . . .

Later

Have been to the library and photocopied Great-Aunt Emma's patent application for the amplitudinal sandstorm generator. Librarian was very reluctant even to unlock the doors for me, as he was busy packing his personal things so he can leave this town like everyone else. But I guess I was convincing when I told him it was a matter of Life and Death.

Not a bad idea, that sandstorm. At the very least, it might keep the construction crews from their work. Maybe. For a while.

I'm back at the El Dungeon now, wondering where I can find an oscillating vortical accelerator and an astrogendetic gyroscope. As well as an ablation shield, a guide wire lumen, and all the other assorted mechanical sundries I will need. Am thinking the junkmail factory is not a bad place to look. Have to wait until dark to try that, though, since there are still a couple of police officers roaming the streets, scavenging the abandoned homes and stores.

In the meantime, I also need a nice, private place to build this thing. Am wondering if that lab coat I found in the secret closet is any kind of clue . . . Great-Aunt Emma WAS an inventor. I just bet she had some kind of laboratory down there. Most likely behind that locked door. Will just have to break in there and check it out.

Later, Much Later

The locks on the door down in the secret closet are tougher than I expected. At first I was really surprised. Not to mention discouraged. Then I remembered whose secret closet this was. Come on. Of course the locks WOULD be tough, but surely Great-Aunt Emma expected that some little great-niece of hers would come along someday and try to open them? And she'd want to let that little great-niece in, I just know it.

The cats and I stood around for a while as I was thinking all this and gazing at the locks and trying to, like, convince them to open through the sheer force of my mind, or Great-Aunt Emma's spirit powers, or something. Absolutely nothing happened, and then I started to feel foolish and thought I might as well take some kind of concrete action toward opening them, instead of standing around like a drooling idiot.

So here's what I've learned:

The top one looks like a straightforward bolt with a basic steel knob, but I can't turn it. I mean, it's really solid, and I've already tried pliers, boltcutters, and a blowtorch. (Local hardware store closed forever=lots of perfectly good, easily fixable tools in Dumpster=paradise.)

The middle one looks like a tiny stoplight. There's a small circle of glass in the door, and red, yellow, and green lights behind it. The yellow light is lit.

The bottom one consists of a row of dials, like the ones on a combination lock, only with letters and spaces, apparently dialed randomly. It looks like this:

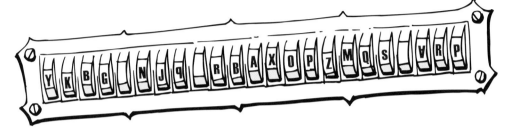

I'm not sure, but I am probably supposed to dial in some code phrase that will open the door.

Have tried OPEN SESAME, PLEASE OPEN THE DOOR, and a few other variations on that theme. Nothing.

Will have to ponder this upstairs. Am expecting a visit from Schneider.

Later

Schneider came into the El Dungeon looking all a-flutter and practically yelling, "I'm the mayor of Blackrock!"

ME:	That was fast.
SCHNEIDER:	Yeah! It was great! The mayor swore me in about an hour ago. Right before he left town.
ME:	Are you sure YOU want to stay? There won't be many buildings standing by tomorrow.

S: That's what I'm here to talk about.

Me: [Noticing Ümlaut's crew listening in.] Let's walk.

[We strolled over to the minipark and continued our powwow in the peace and quiet of the nearly deserted town.]

S: We have a small problem. Everyone knows that Emma LeStrande owns the El Dungeon, but . . . well . . .

Me: Spill.

S: There's no proof.

Me: What?!

S: I don't know. I've looked in all the official records, but there's nothing anywhere that says she owns it.

Me: So . . .

S: At this point anyone with a reasonable claim could take ownership. I guess that's you or Attikol.

Me: What kind of claim does HE have?

S: Money.

Me: Right. Well, who decides?

S: Me, but I need three councilmembers to sign off on my decision. Luckily there are still three left in town. But they've all been approached by Attikol already. I assume they've taken some bribes.

Me: This sucks rocks.

S: Word.

Me: Didn't we have an agreement about you not using teen slang?

S: Sorry. Real sorry about that. Oh, also, one other thing, for what it's worth: I found out for sure that the building got painted beige BEFORE Emma died. Isn't that . . . strange?

ME: It doesn't make any sense.

S: I know.

ME: Unless Emma . . . wow.

S: Yeah, huh?

ME: Wild.

We agreed to meet in three hours at City Hall to see if we could talk the remaining councilmembers into seeing my side of things. Am about to sneak over to the junk-mail factory, to practice my lockpicking and looting skills.

Later

Excellent loot at the factory! Also, am glad that the locks were so much easier to pick than the ones in the secret closet. I now have my oscillating vortical accelerator and astrogendetic gyroscope and everything else I need. Also, it was great fun poking around in the deserted factory. I LOOOOOOOOOOOVE deserted factories! I scored some great cortical snippers, a modulated catheterizing burner, and a really nice heavy-duty fluorescent polarity iron, which might help with Great-Aunt Emma's burly locks. Am really hoping I can get that room open and build my sandstorm generator before my City Hall meeting. Time is a-wasting!

Later

Tried all my fancy new tools on the top bolt, but no dice. And, still NO idea what to do about the other two locks. Had to leave for my meeting at City Hall, so I told Raven to go down into the closet and see if she could muscle that top bolt open. Closed up the café and bailed. Fingers crossed!

Later

Oh frackalacking jabberwocking gramfadiddling . . . uh . . . framcheese!!!!

No swear words can convey my excitement right now, because the El Dungeon is MINE!!

Here's how it went down:

Met Schneider and three councilmembers in the mayor's office (uh, Mayor Schneider's office, that is), and he laid out the situation for them. They were acting all nice and agreeable and VERY sorry that there was nothing they could do for me. First off, even though it was great that I had in my possession a letter from Emma addressing me as her great-niece, there was nothing to prove the letter was actually written to ME. It was also nice how I looked just like her, but that wasn't exactly irrefutable evidence, either. They'd even be willing to let all that slide, if not for the sad fact that, unfortunately, there was nothing, anywhere, in writing to prove Emma actually owned the El Dungeon in the first place.

Then I had a brainwave.

"Park bench," I said to Schneider, and he slapped his forehead.

We mobilized the councilmembers for a quick field trip down to the minipark, where we were able to show them, IN WRITING, in brass letters an inch high, our proof that Emma was indeed the owner of Blackrock's first and only café.

(I did have a moment of terror when I realized the bench now read "Emma LeStrange" and remembered my letter-flipping incident back on Day 6. But then I realized, if they were willing to accept an inscription on a park bench as proof of ownership, one wrong letter wasn't going to be the deal breaker.)

The three of them looked at the bench, nodded, murmured a little legal talk, and then politely mentioned "compensation."

Schneider shook his head. "No more bribes, honorable councilmembers," he said. "It's not going to work like that anymore. Uh, besides which, we've got nothing to offer you."

There was a little more polite legal talk, and then the next thing I knew, everyone was handing around documents, shaking hands, and signing off, and then I was the new legal owner of the El Dungeon, just like that.

"Hey, Schneider," I said when the councilmembers had left us there at the minipark. "What just happened?"

"You got lucky, kid," he said. "Attikol did talk to them about a payoff. But he never came through, and what do you know, rumor has it that he's low on money. So, even though your evidence was kind of pathetic, you really had no competition. So you won this round. But like I've said, I really doubt that a question over legal ownership will keep him from knocking this building over if that's what he wants to do. I hope you have a plan."

Yeah . . . me too.

Later

Poor golem! Poor poor poor poor golem!

I am a very bad golem-commander!

Raven broke all her fingers, wrists, elbows, and shoulders working on that evil bolt down in the closet. Had to work very hard to repair her. Thank goodness for the local deserted hardware store and its well-stocked Dumpsters. She said it did not hurt, but still. Am feeling like a big jerk.

I feel bad for even calling this good news, but she DID get the bolt open. I wish I knew how to reward her.

One down, two more locks to go.

Later

Still no ideas on those locks, but I've built the amplitudinal sandstorm generator as per Aunt Emma's specifications. Since I have no lab to work in, I had to just move aside some furniture and use the El Dungeon. Installed the completed device in the middle of a deserted intersection, just for fun. And cranked it up. Should see

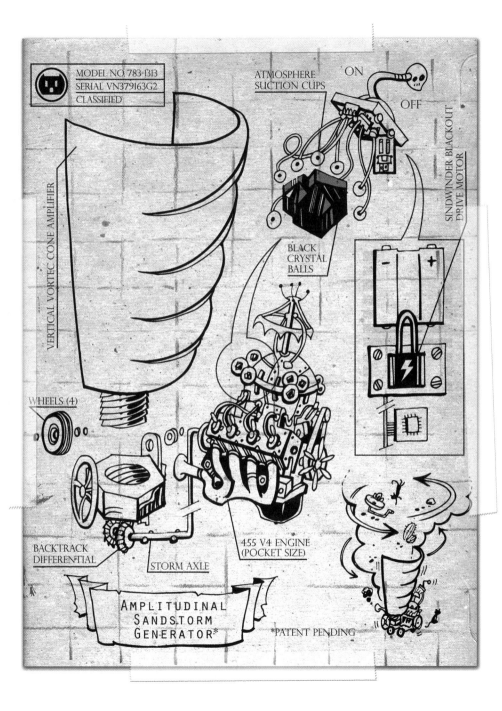

results some time tomorrow. Am going to spend the night pondering the further details of my plan for convincing Attikol to leave here forever.

Day 28

Ümlaut brought me a note from Jakey this morning. Here it is:

What's up Earwig how are you. I would come see you but I am scared to get larginitis. Are you better yet? I am so borred. We havent done a show in like three days because everyone left town. I think we are going to leave town soon too. Attikol is almost done with his chalenge. That bayse building where you are staying is the last one and he will probly get it moved today and then he is going to ask Raven to come with us. And I know you didnt want to come with us last time I asked you but where else are you going to go if you dont have your memery back? And there is going to be nothing left here pretty soon. Well just wanted to say hi or bye or whatever. I hope you are OK

Your ~~frend frend~~ friend Jakey

That was pretty depressing by itself, but then Molly Merriweather marched in with her suitcases and her big smile and her positive, can-do attitude and that made it even worse.

MOLLY: Man, where is everyone? This place is dusted!

ME: Told you not to come.

M: Yeah well, let's solve that mystery of yours so we

can move on to a new town, 'K? And don't worry, I
won't say the code word this time!

ME: [Suddenly unable to breathe.] CODE . . . WORD?
WHAT . . . CODE . . . WORD?

M: The one that made your memory come back. Oh,
right. Of course you don't remember that.

ME: [Ears buzzing. Hands itching to grab Molly and
shake the code word right out of her.] WELL? What
are you waiting for?? Tell it to me right now!!

M: No way, man. You got really mad at me last time.

ME: But . . . I . . . I did?

M: Yeah, you said I was never supposed to know it in
the first place. You made me swear on my ponies
that if I ever saw you again, I wouldn't tell you
your real name, or the code word, or, uh,
whatever other stuff it was you needed to forget.

I put my head in my arms and sent powerful thought waves of
aggravation toward that version of Myself who put me in this
impossible situation. I was vaguely aware of Molly saying a bunch
of "Hey, girl, I'm here for you" and "It's all gonna work out fine."
It was enough to make me promise myself never to show weak-
ness in front of her again.

So I forced myself to recover from my three minutes of despair
and get back to business. Unfortunately, it was not really possible

for me to get back to business with Molly in the picture, asking questions about who was the hottest guy in town, and offering ridiculous non-solutions like "Hey—let's ask Ripper what he thinks we should do!!" Eventually I had to admit defeat. So I made another promise to myself: I would do my best to neutralize whatever crazy plans she came up with, or die trying. Then I handed over my notebook and told her she had an hour to come up with something quality or she was off the case.

At least she's a fast reader. Within twenty minutes of flipping the pages and saying "Hmmm" and "Uh huh, huh," she tossed the notebook back at me.

MOLLY: So, can you program Raven to say whatever?

ME: Probably. Yeah.

M: Well there you go. Just get her to embarrass Attikol in public. You know, insult his manhood or whatever. He'll never show his face here again.

ME: [Very sincerely. Lying my cheeks off.] Molly, thank you. That is an amazing plan. I owe you everything.

M: Hey, no prob! Let's go check out your cool van, huh? We can drive around town and see what's going on.

Fine. Change of scenery. Cats and Molly and Raven and I closed up the café, piled into the van, and rolled out.

We had been in the van only a couple minutes when I heard Raven say, "Sandstorm."

"Huh?"

She pointed off toward the edge of town. "Sandstorm."

She was right, my sandstorm was building up, maybe a mile away. It was nice and easy to see, what with so many of Blackrock's buildings lying in ruins. I thought we'd probably have an hour, maybe two, before it hit us.

We rolled on. I stayed hidden in the back while Molly sat up front and took in the "sights" of Blackrock. That took about three minutes. We had seen all the rubble we needed to see, and were trying to turn down the alley behind the El Dungeon, when we were stopped at a construction roadblock. Molly leaned out the window to chat with the construction crew.

MOLLY:	Whatcha doing?
CONSTRUCTION GUY:	Gettin' paid double time to get this building moved one inch to the east, if you can believe that.
M:	Oh, I believe it. How's it coming?
CG:	Ain't budgin' a lick, is how it's comin'.
M:	Really, why's that? You all look pretty strong.

CG: Well, see this wall here where the paint is chippin'
off? Down where the tractor blade has been workin'
at it? That building is made of solid black . . . I don't
even know, glass or rock or something. Never seen
anything so hard. Broke a drop-forged steel blade off
that tractor. And that's AMERican steel.

M: Aw, that shouldn't stop you for very long.

CG: 'Fraid so, unless we can get some heavier rigs up on in
here.

M: Wow. OK, well, you all stay cool now, you hear?

I wished I could stay cool, but all I wanted to do was chain myself
to the building to keep them from wrecking it. Well, at least they
were stopped for now.

Since we couldn't park at the El Dungeon just yet, we drove on
aimlessly. Suddenly there was this awful howling, I mean
AWFUL, and the sandstorm slapped us like a big heavy sand-hand
out of the sky. Got those windows rolled up fast and stopped the
van, since we couldn't see anything but sand out there anymore.

"Uh, sorry, guys. I didn't think it would hit this fast. We might
be here a while."

"That's cool, why don't we get some good lines written for
Raven?"

I have to say, there is no way I would have come up with the
sort of overblown, drama-dripping, soap-operatic lines Molly

wrote for Raven. Tell you the truth, they were embarrassing: "Stand up and face me like a man," "What of your professed love for me?" "I gave you a challenge. Tell me, how have you fared?" Ugh!!

But who knows? Maybe all that will be just perfect for him. Hey, he's probably never heard Raven say a complete sentence. He'll be lapping it up!

About an hour later

Still in the van, parked in the sandstorm. No sign of it letting up. We are all a little stir-crazy. Cats and Molly are bouncing off the walls. Am trying to distract the cats by tossing bits of wadded-up paper for them to chase, but they are just getting more wound up. I'm afraid it's only a matter of time before one of them needs to use the catbox, which right now is the floor of the van. Am also trying to distract Molly with idle conversation. Pretty torturous

for me since she mainly talks about her hundreds of acquaintances and their various dramas. I did find out one interesting thing: Molly says that after she met me, she went back to my house in Blandindulle, where she was indeed staying with my mom, and looked through all the photo albums there, and get this, our childhood pictures don't look anything alike! So, chances are—and we both like this idea a lot—in a year or so, we won't even look like each other anymore.

"It's like we grew together, and soon we'll grow apart," Molly says, very dramatically.

She also tells me that she has been calling Sharon and George regularly these days. "Just to make sure no one's staying in my room." She looks at me and laughs. "No offense."

Man, I have to solve my problems fast and get Molly out of my hair SOONLIKE. Am waiting very impatiently for the sand to clear up.

About two hours later
BREAKTHROUGH!!!!! (Finally!)

We had all been sitting around in the van for several hours while we waited for the sandstorm to stop. Molly was getting testy, and trying to talk me into sending Raven out into the storm to turn off the generator, which wasn't going to happen. That girl does not take well to boredom. Eventually I had to start giving her assignments. First I tried to get her to write a well-supported descriptive essay on what she did last summer, but she flat-out refused. Then I told her she should talk to Raven for a while, but that made her even crabbier. Finally I told her to look around the van for McFreely's collar and she did give it a shot for about five minutes and then gave up. She informed me she was going crazy and plopped herself down on the backseat of the van nice and hard, which apparently unlatched some sort of latch, causing the seat to spring up violently and pitch Molly face-first onto the floor. When the cats and I got done laughing our cheeks off, I thought to inspect under the seat, which is where I found THE GLORIOUS AMNESIA DEVICES.

Oh lovely. Good old cranky Molly. Good old amnesia devices! I wanted to hug them. Uh, unfortunately there is no RESTORE device. Or maybe it's fortunate, since I really don't know if I would've had the self-control to maintain my amnesia for one more minute. Instead, there's a BACKUP device and a BLOCK device, which has several dials where you can set expiration dates

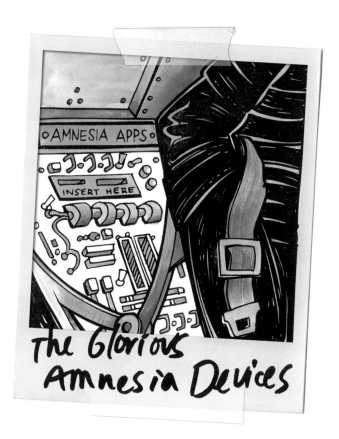

The Glorious
Amnesia Devices

for several different cases of amnesia. (Which gives me ideas. But more on that later.) My own current case of the forgetfulness is going to clear up in two days. Which, according to Molly, is when my mom expects me home.

Am extremely happy to know there is a solid expiration date on the amnesia.

Now if we could just get out of the van.

About an hour later

Sandstorm is over. We are all walking around, overjoyed to be out of the van. Also, the sandstorm scoured all the beige off Emma's building. Belgium, it's AMAZING! Those old photos I saw were of a plain, reasonably attractive black building, nothing extraordinary at all. But now, what I'm seeing? It's a different ANIMAL. I mean, it's actually kind of LIKE an animal. It has scaly texture and ridges and a crazy sort of beak on the roof. Weird curvy pillars, sinister carved plants and animals and ghoulish faces, gargoyles frolicking on the roof and hanging off the corners. And when I say frolicking, I mean I can see them kind of just out the corner of my eye, darting around, and then dashing back to their places when I look. And all in slick, glistening, harder-than-drop-forged-American-steel black rock.

Weird, huh?

I wonder what made it change since the old photos?

At least I'm pretty sure I understand the beigeifying now. If I were Great-Aunt Emma, I'd be pretty anxious to keep this place hidden from certain eyes.

Um, I AM pretty anxious to keep this place hidden from certain eyes, and I don't have any three-story beige dropcloths handy, either.

There is now nothing left standing in Blackrock except Emma's building. Therefore, it's pretty easy to see out to the edge of town, where Professor Ümlaut's Prophylactery and Revue and

Uncle Attikol's Deadly Dollhouse are still hanging around, in trailers that are very ready for new post-sandstorm paint jobs.

Showdown time is coming.

Day 29

Am sitting on the bench at the minipark. Have talked to Molly about that code word of hers. She says it was just something my mom said a lot, so when I found Molly in Blandindulle, she naturally said it to me. I guess I had set it up as a sort of failsafe, in case something went terribly wrong, so that my mom would be able to break the amnesia.

Anyway, I sent Molly down into the closet to try entering the code word in the bottom lock. Then left her and Raven at the El Dungeon, which is currently full of construction workers getting coffee and sandwiches before they ditch town. Word is, they are giving up. All their equipment has been wrecked on my crazy black building and in the sandstorm. Attikol doesn't have the money to keep them here, or the manpower to threaten them all with kneecapping, so that's that—looks like he is not going to be completing his challenge after all.

Not that he isn't still a major threat to me. If I don't get him thoroughly neutralized, he will eventually be back with more money and more construction crews with bigger equipment.

Have been sitting here on the bench pondering all this, plotting my next move, and staring at the ex-tree, which as of yesterday was the only tree left in Blackrock, but after yesterday's sandstorm is a lifeless, leafless, barkless, branchless trunk. Was feeling kind of bad that I had to go and destroy the very last tree in Blackrock, but the more I looked at it, the less it looked like an ex-tree at all, and the more it looked like a too-smooth, too-round, human-made, tree-simulating POLE. With a scar near the base, where someone apparently tried (and failed) to cut it down. Its "knothole," about five feet up, is so clearly a button, I wonder how I ever mistook it for a knothole.

Thought back to Day 6, when I hit that button with a rock, and the letter in the bench flipped over, and my innocent young heart was filled with dreams of glorious secret contraptions all through the town. Man, why couldn't the locks downstairs work that easily?

Oh wait now.

The light on the middle lock was yellow. Not red.

Maybe I've already done something to turn it yellow.

—OK, have given the button another hit with a rock, and maybe—

Hey, I see Molly running up, gotta go

Later—oh this is goooooood stuff!

OK: Molly told me something amazing: She dialed in her code word, and then the dials started turning on their own!!!!!

She and I ran down into the closet right away.

First thing I noticed was that the dials had indeed changed.

Second thing was that the light on the middle lock was green. And the lock was open. Sweet—Looks like the ex-tree button did the trick!

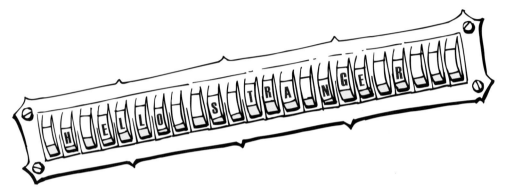

Third thing was that the bottom lock was still locked.

So. I sent Molly back upstairs and I'm at the door right now.

Having some kind of conversation.

With the ghost in the door.

First I dialed "HELLO GREAT-AUNT EMMA."

And watched in creeped-out amazement as the dials turned on their own to say "WELCOME MY DEAR."

ME:	MAY I COME IN
GREAT-AUNT EMMA:	IS YOUR FRIEND GONE
ME:	YES

```
GAE:  HOW DID SHE KNOW CODE
ME:   FROM MY MOM
GAE:  I HOPE YOU TRUST HER
ME:   ME TOO
GAE:  ARE YOU READY
ME:   AHAHAHHAHAHAHHAHAHAHHHA
GAE:  BE SERIOUS
ME:   IM VERY SERIOUS
GAE:  I KNOW
```

And the door clicked open.

I think I was expecting to see Great-Aunt Emma. But the room is empty. Of ghosts, I mean. It's full of shelves and shelves holding jars of black rock. Jars that have dates on them. Dates that go back CENTURIES. And notebooks. Notebooks full of detailed information on centuries' worth of experiments.

Holy

Experiments involving the black rock.

And behind the shelves, on all the walls, and even on the ceiling, tiny handwriting. I still have MUCH more to read, but here's what I learned in the past half hour:

1. Hundreds of years ago, my family and Attikol's were in a bitter feud that had been raging on for decades.

2. They were feuding over ownership of the liquid black rock, which both families believed to have amazing and . . . unusual properties.

3. My family had been using it mainly for scientific-experimentation-type purposes, whereas Attikol's family had been selling it as a cure-all in their traveling medicine show.

4. Sometime in the 1620s, my family won the rights to the black rock in an epic game of Primero Calamità, which was a VERY early version of . . . that's right. Calamity Poker.

5. Attikol's family stood by the

Blackrock !

outcome of that game for about 200 years.

6. But during that time, Attikol's family legend was getting more and more . . . fictionalized.

7. So by the time Attikol's great-great-great-grandjerk started up the feud again, he didn't even know what they had actually been fighting over, 200 years prior.

8. And by the time the family Destiny had been handed down to Attikol, the story had been completely mangled. Like a game of Operator played over 400 years. By a bunch of half-wits.

9. So Attikol doesn't know Great-Aunt Emma was his ancestral enemy. He just started coming to Blackrock about 13 years ago because he liked it here. Town officials easily bribed, good audiences for the gun and doll show, great Pötion sales, etc.

10. But Great-Aunt Emma had been keeping tabs on him, and when she saw that he was headed to Blackrock, she beigeified the El Dungeon, to disguise it.

11. And then made her arrangements to have letters sent to me and Schneider 13 years later.

12. And then died.

13. And it goes to show just how bright Attikol is, that all these years later, and even with the Moon Child working for him, he still doesn't have a clue.

Pretty great stuff, huh? I may not know my real name, but I'm busting with family pride.

Also, I am now more worried than ever about Attikol seeing Emma's building without its protective beigeifications.

Also, I have a crazy, possibly desperate idea how to get rid of Attikol once and for all.

Later

Molly had already made friends with all the construction workers at the El Dungeon and was getting antsy, so I took her upstairs with me to pay Schneider a visit at Crazy Vet Hilda's. The two of them were drinking tea in her kitchen. And being crawled over by 13 or so former alley cats. And having a conversation. It's beyond me how he can understand her. Clearly a case of hereditary mental oddness.

As soon as we came in she started on the nonsense.

HILDA: Flu loathe book must bite cold lemming!

ME: Yes, it . . . must.

SCHNEIDER: She says you both look just like old Emma. Wow, Earwig, I didn't know you had a twin. Is she named after an insect, too?

ME: That's very witty, Schneider. Molly, meet Mayor Schneider, professional laugh riot.

H: Postmark brewery ghoul seems adverbial!

ME: Totally adverbial . . . Hey, Molly, why don't you go upstairs with Hilda and take the tour? . . . So, listen, Schneider. I really need to ask you one last favor. You know how to play Calamity Poker?

S: Oh no, I could never afford to play even one game.

ME: Well that's great, because . . . wait, what?

S: I've never played it. Anyway, it takes years to learn all the rules.

ME: No way, man, I learned it in a few days.

S: What? Who taught you? I heard you have to go through some kind of blood ritual first, so you can be an honorary relative of Attikol's.

ME: Ewwwwwwwwwww!

S: Sorry, that's what I heard. I guess he takes that game really seriously.

ME: Well listen. How would you like to become an honorary member of MY family?

S: Sure. Wait, does it involve a blood ritual?

ME: No. Well, that WOULD be kind of cool actually.

S: Didn't I just hear you ewwing at blood rituals?

ME: Oh no. I was ewwing at becoming a relative of Attikol's.

S: Oh, right. But how come your family is allowed to learn Calamity Poker?

ME: Well that's a story for another time, isn't it? Anyway, I hereby declare you an honorary relative of Emma LeStrande, and of me, Earwig, whatever my last name may be, from now until eternity, across the known universe, yeah yeah yeah, so be it.

S: Sounds good. Now do you mind just explaining what is going on?

ME: You're gonna be the Dealer at a very important game of Calamity Poker. Here [handing him <u>The LeStrande Guide to Calamity Poker</u>, copyright 1890, which I'd found in the secret closet], start learning the rules, I'll be back.

Later

Some stuff has happened. Major stuff. Not a lot of time right now, but am feeling the need to document EVERYTHING in these critical moments. Here goes.

When Molly and I got back to the El Dungeon, I told her I needed to talk to her out in the van. And when we got in there I pointed at the amnesia devices and said, "How would you like to be a completely new person for the next three months?"

MOLLY: [Flabbergasted.] Are you even kidding me right now?

ME: Amnesia device is right here, Molly. I can set it for three months. Six months, a year. Ride of your life, I guarantee it.

M: [Eyes totally glowing.] You are not even kidding me right now.

ME: Let's get your suitcases and see if you have anything that looks like my dress, huh?

It took her about half an hour to get herself outfitted into a reasonable copy of me. I trimmed her bangs. Found her a mostly blank notebook in the Dumpster near the school. And wrote her a cheat sheet. It went a little something like this:

- Your name is Earwig.
- You have a friend named Jakey who is a for real psychic.
- You have to go find his trailer and tell him what happened, which is that you fell and hit your head and started losing all your memories for the third time, so you started writing this note so you would know what to do after everything was gone.
- And now everything is gone.

I figure she can let Jakey fill in the rest of the blanks for her. I just really hope that she can keep him busy while I play a quick game of Calamity Poker with Attikol.

Later

Things are moving along nicely. Made some preparations, got Raven all programmed for her role in the plan, then the cats and I went and knocked on Jakey's trailer. Boy was he surprised to see me! And even more surprised when I told him I wanted to join the medicine show. Said I'd be the crystal ball reader. Told him I'd missed him a lot—at least that part was true.

And guess what—it worked, my plan with the cats, to keep Jakey from reading my mind. I got the idea from Great-Aunt Emma's patent application for the Cat Thoughtwave Amplifier. She had found that just a small dollop of liquid black rock could amplify the thoughts of cats to the point that any ordinary human could understand them. I figured, if I cranked the volume on the cats' thoughts, they'd be so loud that Jakey wouldn't know what was really on my mind. Especially if I distracted him with stuff he really wanted to hear. Anyway, it worked! I gave the cats a good soaking in black rock and could hardly hear myself think.

I'll admit, I wasn't sure it would work. Wouldn't have taken the risk at all if I didn't think it was necessary. I thought and thought about it, and what it came down to was this: I just didn't believe Jakey would take me/Molly along with the caravan unless he'd heard it from me that I wanted to come. You know? Still, I had severe doubts about going over there. I'd even thought about wearing a cap of tinfoil. Thought very seriously about it. But in the end I didn't. I mean, either the black-rock-soaked cats would do the trick, or they wouldn't. Also, I don't know that there have been, like, a bunch of well-documented studies showing that tinfoil is effective at blocking mental attacks or psychic leakage.

Anyway, the cats DID do the trick. Poor Jakey, he was just listening to their crazy thoughts (mostly evil intentions toward his parrot), and never noticed me lying my cheeks off. I do feel kinda bad for tricking him. Even if it's for my Destiny and all. But you know what, Molly will be a much better friend for him than I would. I can only stand human company for so long.

He seemed so happy about me coming with them, though.

I have a feeling that's going to haunt me.

Day 30

Molly Merriweather may not be good with boredom, but at least she's up for an adventure. I had Raven drive us all out to the medicine show caravan, and then I gave Molly a nice tough case of amnesia with an expiration date of three months. That should get them far enough away. Quickly, before the dazed look in her eyes could clear up, I handed her the cheat sheet and the blank notebook, and pointed her toward Jakey's trailer.

Then I hid in the van and waited until Raven said Molly was inside. And then Raven and I went to see Attikol.

All the fashionistas were running around packing up their medicines, guns, dolls, crystal balls, and what-have-you. General moving-day hubbub: shouts of "Pinking screamcakes!" and "Blood and Gor!" Curls was toting boxes and swearing. No Attikol (or Ümlaut) in sight. The bosses were apparently kicking back while the underlings broke camp. We found their trailers—not hard, they had large lurid (though partially sand-blasted) portraits of Attikol and Ümlaut painted on the sides—and Raven knocked on Attikol's door.

I stood beside her and kept a half-eye on Jakey's trailer. I wanted—needed—his door to stay shut.

Attikol looked uncomfortable seeing us. I guess he's not in a very good position as regards Raven right about now. Seeing as there is still a building left in its original position.

ATTIKOL: Raven, my darling. I was just on my way to see you.

RAVEN: Attikol. I know you have not yet fulfilled your challenge.

A: Wha . . . ? Did you just . . . say a complete sentence?

R: Attikol, you must prove your love! You must!

A: Yeah, yeah, this is exciting. I've never seen you like this, darling.

[Medicine show personnel were freezing in their tracks and staring at us. Just what I'd hoped for.]

R: I have had a change of heart. My first challenge was far too destructive. In lieu of moving the last building in Blackrock an inch to the east, I challenge you to a game of Calamity Poker.

[Gun and doll show staff were glancing at one another and laughing nervously.]

A: Raven, surely you're having a little joke with me. You would have to endure a terrifying blood ritual to become my honorary relative—and that's just to learn the rules. It takes years to develop the kind of subtle talent you'd need to win a game against ME.

[Just then, Ümlaut threw open his trailer window and leaned out, yelling at Attikol.]

Ü: Come on, Attikol, we all know you're just broke. Gor, I'll lend you the money myself! Don't act like you're afraid to play her!

[I stared nervously at Jakey's trailer, but it was probably pretty normal for Ümlaut and Attikol to scream at each other like that . . . anyway, Jakey's door didn't open.]

R: Say you'll play just one game with me, Attikol. I don't have to be your relative to play, do I?

A: . . . No.

R: I wouldn't want to be your relative anyway, would I? It might . . . get in our way . . . later.

A: RAWR! Now you're talking!

R: Excellent. Choose your partner and meet us at the El Dungeon in one hour.

A: Wait, who will be your partner?

R: My assistant, Earwig, will play with me.

A: [Looking extremely pleased.] What a charming idea, my charming charming darling. And the Dealer?

R: The mayor of Blackrock has agreed to play that role.

A: [Looking like he could not believe his luck.] He's still here? Wonderful. Marvelous. I'll see you, ladies, in one hour.

An hour later

Attikol, Ümlaut, and their crew have just arrived at the El Dungeon. I was standing outside with Schneider, assuring him he should just be an impartial judge, follow the rules, and not interfere—just like Great-Aunt Emma told him in her letter. Anyway, Attikol REALLY made me nervous when he walked up. I guess it was the first time he'd seen the El D. since the beige came off. He came right up close to the wall, touched it, and tried scratching it with a fingernail. My heart was sure beating. But he didn't say anything, just went inside with the others.

I was surprised to see Curls with them, but I was stunned when he sat down next to Attikol at the gaming table. I kind of expected Attikol would knock him out of the chair for that faux pas . . . but nope, it looks like Curls is going to be Attikol's partner. Am trying to see if he looks pale or anything. You know, from the terrifying blood ritual. Wonder what Attikol is thinking, having Curls be his partner? Ehh, he's probably just trying to look gallant for Raven. Like he's SOOOO not worried he'll win. We will see.

Am scribbling this behind the counter while everyone gets espresso and makes nice-nice with one another. Will have to write more later—things are about to heat up.

Later

Game is progressing slowly. Luckily, all eyes are on Attikol and Raven, and no one expects me to care about the outcome of the game. So no one minds that I'm writing madly in my notebook at the gaming table. I have lots of time while Attikol and Schneider discuss historical precedents, relevant contingencies, and the laws and bylaws of Calamity Poker scoring. Am trying not to worry about the fairly inevitable conclusion that we are going to lose this game.

Am relying on my instincts to get us through this no matter what happens.

OK. The action so far:

Schneider called the room to order. Attikol looked a little surprised to find it was Schneider, and not his buddy the former mayor, who was overseeing the game, but what was he going to do about it? And everything pointed to him winning anyway. Since he is the only one of us who has ever actually played the game.

Schneider put my copy of <u>The LeStrande Guide to Calamity Poker</u> on the table and announced that today's game would follow the rules of gameplay and scoring as set down in the book.

Attikol looked shocked when the book came out, and flipped through it with an expression of disbelief. "Where did this come from?" And then, under his breath: "As far as I knew, MY family wrote the only existing rulebook."

I spoke up. "I, uh, found it in the Dumpster behind the library. Sir."

Attikol laughed. "Fine. These rules are good enough. Showdown style, I presume? How many rounds?"

We all agreed on a 13-round game, which made me feel pretty lucky. Then just as we were about to get down to some serious card playing, Attikol stood up.

He cleared his throat and said to the whole room, "Thank you all for being gathered here today to witness this momentous occasion. As you know, I am here to honor my darling Raven's . . . request . . . that I prove my love by besting her and her charming assistant, Earwig, in a game of Calamity Poker. A game that I take very seriously. Four hundred years ago, my ancestors won their vast riches in a game of Calamity Poker played against a corrupt tribe of magicians, who had been tormenting the local villagers, ruining their crops, killing their cattle, and so on . . . My noble forefathers restored honor to the villagers and burned the magicians—all but one treacherous survivor, who stole the secret source of my family's great Mystical Power. After today, I will continue my Destiny to seek and win back that secret source of power . . . with the lovely Raven at my side. Let us all agree that we will stand by the rulings of our honorable judge and Dealer, Mayor Schneider. Let the game commence!"

My eyes were watering with the strain of not laughing. Hand was cramping with the strain of getting it all down on paper. Most of the audience was yawning. The game commenced.

Calamity Poker, as I learned earlier today from studying The LeStrande Guide, can be played Casual style or Showdown style. Casual style, which the Ümlaut crew always played, consists of as many rounds as the players feel like playing, with no ultimate winner per se, just a redistribution of wealth. In Showdown style, players agree to a certain number of rounds. The Dealer determines which team wins each round. (In our case, best of 13 rounds would win the Showdown.) Betting during the game determines what the players actually win or lose. If your hand leads the round, you can either take the pot of money, choose some other reward (subject to the Dealer's approval), or stipulate a consequence of the ultimate win—some condition that the losing team would have to accept.

I had handed my camera to one of the fashionistas to get our picture once we started playing. Here it is:

The Gaming table.

Anyway. Here's how the game has gone so far:

ROUND 1: Much tension when it looked like I would actually win the first hand, but then Attikol pointed out a little-known point bonus for the rare combination of suits in his hand, and Schneider agreed. Attikol chose to stipulate a consequence of the ultimate win: If he won, Raven would join the caravan and leave with him.

ROUND 2: Attikol's hand was the clear winner. He chose to kiss Raven's hand. Weirdo.

ROUND 3: My hand and Attikol's tied. We went into a challenge round. Being on the losing team, I got to assign the challenge. Attikol picked Embarrassing Truth, and I asked him, "Isn't it true that you once wore women's underpants on your head when no other hat was available?" He said no, but you could hardly hear him over the raucous laughter. Citing the 1886 Convention on Audience Laughter, Schneider ruled that I had led the hand, and I chose to stipulate: If we won, I would get to join the caravan. Clearly this came out of left field for Attikol, but he made a face like "Kids—who can understand them?" and we carried on.

ROUND 4: Curls' hand led. He chose to take the pot of money. Attikol was obviously annoyed.

ROUND 5: My hand led. I chose to stipulate: If we lost, I would get to join the caravan. Head-scratching all around. Attikol shrugged and said, "OK, kid, guess you've got your bases covered."

ROUND 6: Raven's hand led. She chose to stipulate: If Attikol's side won, she and I would both join the caravan, and Attikol would win her heart—but they must never return to Blackrock again, because it would remind her too much of her pathetic existence before Attikol. Big smiles from Attikol.

ROUND 7: Raven's hand led. She chose to stipulate: Due to her tender feelings for Attikol, if he failed her second challenge, she would lose so much respect for him that she must insist that he never return to Blackrock. Attikol put on a noble-concerned face, but I felt he was getting a little anxious. And we were now up by one hand.

ROUND 8: Very close round, but Attikol managed to lead it, finally convincing Schneider that, considering our position in the lunar cycle, Rule 456.2.9 took clear precedence over Rule J78.43. He chose to request a 30-minute intermission for coffee. Schneider approved it. We took a break.

Later

Am worried at the way things are headed. Very worried.

"Keep an ear on Attikol," I whispered to Raven as she went behind the counter to make espresso. Attikol, meanwhile, seemed to be idly chatting with his crew, but in a minute or two I saw one of them, a tall guy in a vintage fedora, casually slip out the door.

I hunkered down next to Raven's stool and whispered to her.

ME: Raven, please tell me your ears are bionic.

Raven: My ears are bionic.

ME: I hope you're not just saying that. Did you hear what Attikol said to Vintage Fedora Guy?

R: He said, "Get Jakey."

SWEARWORD!! I had to intercept Vintage Fedora Guy somehow. Yes. Somehow.

I stood up. Ümlaut was on the other side of the counter, waiting for his cappuccino and looking glum.

I was desperate.

ME: Hey, Ümlaut. How'd you like to do me a very small favor? I'll, uh, put in a good word for you with Raven.

ÜMLAUT: Want me to cheat or something? Tell you Attikol's cards? Not going to happen.

ME: Nothing like that. Just go keep that tall guy, the one in the vintage fedora, away from Jakey's trailer.

Ü: What's this all about?

ME: Oh . . . I . . . [Nuggets! Could not think of anything.] I . . . uh, this is kind of awkward . . .

Ü: Spit it out, kid.

[Frantically I thought, "What would Molly do?" And then I knew.]

> ME: I just don't want Jakey to know . . . that . . . [Taking a deep breath. Feeling unspeakably dirty.] I have feelings for Curls. Because Jakey . . . cares about me, and . . . you know, he's so young, and so sensitive . . . I want to tell him myself . . . I don't want him to have to see it in someone else's mind. I know YOU understand. Right?

[Right. An extremely sappy look came over Ümlaut's face.]

> Ü: Yeah, kid, I know. Love . . . hurts. It hurts! Look, don't worry about a thing. I'll take care of it.

And he hustled out without his cappuccino.

Fingers crossed (story of my life as I know it), I went back to the gaming table, trying to console myself that I hadn't exactly LIED. I mean, I DO have feelings for Curls. Feelings of annoyance and irritation, mainly, spiked with occasional pangs of pity.

Later

Coffee break has just ended. No sign of Jakey, Ümlaut, or Vintage Fedora Guy. Our game commenced.

ROUND 9: Curls' hand led. And all because Schneider overlooked Rule 78.b.9, governing the fluctuation of point value in

the Ruby suit in conjunction with the Royal Pickaxe. I thought about speaking up, but in the end, I decided it wasn't worth letting Attikol know I had any interest in the game. Curls went for the money again. Attikol gave him a mighty glaring. I guess Curls doesn't care too much about the health of his kneecaps.

ROUND 10: Attikol's hand led. He chose to stipulate: If he won, he and Raven would be married within a week. Raven gave him a spot-on sweet, demure smile. I congratulated myself for some first-rate programming.

ROUND 11: Raven's hand led. She chose to whisper in Attikol's ear. I don't know what she said, but I bet it was one of Molly's lines, cuz it sure made him blush.

Round 12: Raven's hand led. She chose to give Attikol a kiss on the cheek. He was in heaven.

ROUND 13: I was dealt the rare Blank Slate card, which allowed me to choose the suit and value of the card. Had to ponder it quite a bit before I decided to draw in the symbol for the 13 of Crows, hoping that wouldn't make Attikol too suspicious, even though he would immediately notice the point bonus I would earn in combination with my other card and those on the table.

Like I expected, there was a pretty furious debate when I laid it down, but in the end, when all possible points were tallied and re-tallied, and Attikol had run out of alternate interpretations to argue, Schneider ruled that Curls' hand and mine had tied. I graciously offered to let Curls assign the challenge, and he accepted. I picked Feats of Strength, Skill, and Endurance. And Curls gave us our challenge: Raven would have to fly from the roof of the El Dungeon, or we'd forfeit the round. And therefore the game.

Stunned silence, and then laughter, backslapping, and a general release of tension, as everyone in the room assumed victory was Attikol's.

SCHNEIDER: [Looking mournful.] Raven and Earwig, Rule 20.c.34 clearly states that ALL challenges must be met, no matter how difficult, or you must forfeit the round.

ME: It's OK.

RAVEN: [Nice and loud.] I accept the challenge!

ATTIKOL: You can't! Raven, darling, you don't need to.

R: I accept the challenge!

ME: [To Schneider.] I guess she's accepting the challenge.

S: I think she's . . . confused. Or . . . maybe I'M confused. I don't really know if you want to win or lose, but if she tries the challenge, she's probably going to . . . [Drawing his finger across his neck.]

ME: [Shrugging.] It's her call. I'm just her assistant.

Amid general confusion, low-level panic, and loud complaints, everyone relocated outside except for Raven, who appeared a few minutes later on the roof. Attikol was smacking Curls about the head and neck, growling threats on his life if anything happened to Raven. And still no Ümlaut, Jakey, or Vintage Fedora Guy in sight.

Raven stood at the edge of the roof, three stories up. My hands were sweating. I kept thinking about how she said it didn't hurt when all the bones in her arms were crushed. I kept thinking, "I can rebuild her." I kept thinking, "Should I stop her? What is my plan? Do I HAVE a plan?"

It was windy up there, three stories high. Raven's long wig streamed out behind her, and her skirt and cape billowed and whipped. It was all very dramatic.

She just stood there. And suddenly I had a terrible thought.

What if Raven COULD fly?

We would win the game, and Attikol would have to leave Blackrock forever, but . . . Wouldn't Attikol then suspect her of being his ancestral enemy?

Was Attikol smart enough to suspect her?

Was Attikol too smitten to care?

Raven stood there at the edge of the roof. As if waiting for instructions.

Just then Ümlaut staggered up to me. He'd been in a fight, it looked like—bloody nose, cuts on his cheekbones and eyebrows,

red splotches
that would soon
be bruises, and
a missing tooth.
Clothes all torn up
and dirtied. He grinned
at me and gave me a
thumbs-up. "You're
all good," he said. "Your
Fedora Guy—he never
made it to Jakey."

I pointed wordlessly up at
Raven, and watched the blood
drain out of Ümlaut's face.
Several of his friends promptly
started competing to tell him the
events of the past hour, and it
looked like he was ready to do
some more fighting, if he could
decide whom to fight; but none
of that mattered, because good
or bad, I'd made my decision.

I stepped forward out of the
crowd and yelled up, "FLY, RAVEN, FLY!"

She threw back her arms and leaped into the air.

Half of the crowd covered their eyes. The other half looked down, where they expected her to come crashing to the ground. Schneider and Ümlaut and I kept our eyes on Raven. We saw her rise gracefully off the roof and up into the air. We saw her pirouette and dive. We saw her do majestic, soaring figure eights in midair. And once everyone had seen, and the whole crowd was gasping, and swearing, and calling on their ancestors for deliverance, she came elegantly back down to earth and lighted on the ground in front of Attikol.

ATTIKOL: Darling?

RAVEN: Attikol.

A: [Falling to his knees in front of her.] Give me another chance!

R: Stand up and face me like a man! I have given you two challenges, Attikol. Tell me, how have you fared?

A: I . . . moved all those buildings for you . . . darling?

R: [Sweeping her arm out to indicate what we could all see: the El Dungeon, standing firm on its foundations.] Attikol! [In a voice that wasn't exactly LOUD, but still, a voice I could imagine his ancestors hearing in the depths of hell.] You . . . have . . . FAILED!

Attikol cringed.

GGAWWRKK!!

Then Raven opened her mouth wide in a strange, inhuman way.

And from somewhere deep inside her came this appalling, horrendous bird cry.

I started to sweat again. This wasn't in the programming. Was she breaking down? I really hoped our big dramatic showdown wasn't going to end with me performing an emergency tune-up on her.

Then she started flapping her arms, still making the horrible bird cry. And now there was another commotion in the crowd—in a moment I knew why, because there was a second bird cry, and a big white parrot came flying straight for Raven from the direction of the caravan.

That's when I noticed the strange dark clouds rolling in. Dark clouds . . . with wings in them. And beady eyes. Huge dark clouds of birds.

Jakey's parrot (man, I wish I had asked her name . . .) was the first bird to reach Raven and Attikol. She wheeled around in the air a few feet over Attikol's head as he cowered like the big man he was. She gave this terrible parrot-battle-call . . . and pooped on his shirt.

All the other birds were close behind her, and everyone else had noticed them too, and they were all standing around looking up at the sky . . . with their MOUTHS OPEN . . . like a bunch of dummies, until someone yelled "RUN" and everyone started scattering, though not before a lot of very fine clothing was ruined with bird dooky. I found some shelter in the doorway of the El D., and stood there with Schneider, watching Attikol get PLASTERED with caca, and loving every minute of it.

Right in the thick of the running, and the screaming, and the cawing, and the defecating, Raven spoke to Attikol one last time.

"Leave this town," she said, "and never return."

Attikol turned to go. No inch of him had escaped the poopstorm. He looked back at Raven for a moment, then trudged off to his caravan, a large flock of birds following him all the way.

I forgot for a second that he was my ancestral enemy, and felt kinda bad for him; then I consoled myself that bird poop brings good luck.

Later

Raven and I are hanging out in the El Dungeon by ourselves. Ümlaut has just finished saying his farewells to Raven and is on his sorry way.

He was covered in blood and 20 or 30 birdsplats, but compared with Attikol he looked well-groomed. "Raven," he said, all mournful-like, with anguished love in his eyes, "is there . . . do I . . . can't we . . ."

"No, Ümlaut. Not now. But Earwig will be joining your caravan. Keep an eye on her for me, and maybe someday . . ."

Sheesh! Sappy old golem.

Later

Note to Self: Just because you may have an . . . unusual . . . secret closet that makes sleeping and eating unnecessary doesn't mean you should stop sleeping and eating.

Went and crashed out in

the van in great emotional exhaustion, and slept for the first time in, wow, a whole week. Had an excellent dream about the secret closet. It involved the four black cat statues coming to life, frolicking around on the staircase, pulling up the bucket, riding the black rock waves . . . all the stuff I like to do down there. Also, I had a nice long dream-talk with one of Great-Aunt Emma's portraits. (I may have forgotten to mention it—but Schneider rescued the paintings before the library and City Hall went down, and now both are hanging in the El Dungeon.)

I don't actually recall anything we said, but I think she's pleased with me.

And then I woke up and went into the café for some excellent victory sandwiches with Raven, Hilda, and Schneider. Then we took care of some important town business. Mayor Schneider now has three new councilmembers (Raven, Hilda, and me). Our first official act was to declare it illegal to construct any further buildings in Blackrock.

Good old Schneider. He started to bring up the whole flying incident, but I stopped him with a quick "Ask Great-Aunt Emma." He seemed to understand. Then I asked him to get in touch with me right away if he saw any sign of Attikol, who may be a little dim, but is bound to get suspicious about the flying sooner or later.

Finally I told Schneider he should move into the Old Museum if he wanted, and he said he already had. Ha! That guy is very mental.

Later

Something extremely strange is happening in Blackrock! There are TREES, really weird beautiful black trees, coming up everywhere. They're growing so fast you can actually see it happening. And there are birds in all the trees. Man, Blackrock was missing birds in a big way. But they're here now, loud as can be. My cats are in a shivering, chattering frenzy over it. And are not being allowed outside the El Dungeon right now.

I really don't know how to explain these trees to myself, so I'm going to try to be content with, "Ask Great-Aunt Emma."

Good
Stuff.

Later

I'll give you one guess who sauntered into the El Dungeon an hour ago to take her old job back! Rachel! She doesn't seem at all fazed by the, uh, changes in Blackrock. She is unbelievably perky. She says she mailed all the postcards I gave her, as instructed; met lots of dashing men; got sunburned; dropped her camera in the ocean; ate lots of shrimps off the barby; etc., etc. She is very grateful to me for the cruise. She loooooooves the new furniture in the El D. and thinks we should redecorate the whole place. And she brought her favorite customers souvenir bobblehead koala bears. All of which she gave to me.

Rachel wears me out. I went and hid in the van seven minutes after she arrived. One good thing about her, though: She may be three times my age, but she knows I'm the boss. Great-Aunt Emma must have sent her a letter, too.

Did I mention I still have the amnesia? Am not too worried, though. Today's the expiration date, and I have just about four hours left until midnight.

Later

As tolerable as Blackrock has gotten in the last day or so, I am really craving HOME, so I'm getting prepared to hit the road just as soon as I know which road to hit.

Have taken a last walk around Blackrock, saying goodbye. (For now.) Bottled up a big jar of liquid rock for home experiments—

am excited to see what new uses I can invent for it! Sat on the Emma LeStrange bench at the minipark for a bit listening to birdcalls, and said goodbye to Schneider and Hilda.

I'll miss them.

This sounds crazy, even to me—but I think I've enjoyed being Earwig.

All the same, I am also very anxious to be myself again, so at a quarter till midnight, Raven and I packed up the van, assured Rachel we'd be back in a few months or so, loaded up the cats, and drove away.

Five minutes later

Parked on the side of the road outside Blackrock. Killing time until memory returns. Have interrogated Raven about yesterday's hijinks. Unfortunately (or fortunately? I can't really decide) she is back to minimal conversation skills. Our talk went a little bit like this:

ME: So, Raven.

RAVEN: Yes?

ME: Nice showdown yesterday.

R: Thanks.

ME: What was up with calling all those birds?

R: Iono.

ME: I mean, I didn't program that. What gave you the idea?

R: Iono.

ME: C'mon, did you and Jakey's parrot plan that together?

R: Uhhhhh . . . no.

ME: So . . . seriously, what gives? I thought you were, like, under my control, and here you're calling down epic poopy revenge from the skies on Attikol, and making Ümlaut think he has a chance with you, and NONE of that was in your programming.

R: Uhhhhhh?

So, I don't know. Maybe she's playing dumb. I don't know if I should punish her or reward her or both or neither. Maybe I should just be thankful we got Attikol out of our lives, and leave it at that.

Later—still parked outside Blackrock. Three minutes till midnight.

Not sure if I am feeling funny because my memories are about to return, or if I am just about to vomit out of nervousness that my memories are never returning, after all.

Am trying really hard to think of what my house looks like. So far, noth—

Oh wait

Oh man oh man oh man gonna have to stop writing in a minute here it comes it is all coming back OH YEEEEEEEEEEEEEAHHHH

About twenty minutes—twenty lifetimes later— on the road, heading toward home!

Have recovered somewhat from massive, delicious, inundating influx of life memories. Man, it is soooooooooo goooooooooooood to be ME again.

Also, am EXTREMELY grateful that the Moon Child is miles away, because there is no doubt whatsoever that I'm Attikol's ancestral enemy. And a very . . . UNUSUAL enemy, indeed.

I might even say . . . STRANGE.

Later—AT HOME!!!! YES!!!!!!!!!!!!!!!!!

Things I like best about home:

1. Mom.
2. Mom, for not questioning the fact that my only souvenirs from a month-long cruise to Australia were 15 bobblehead koala bears and a jar of tar.
3. Mom, for making sandwiches that are even better than Raven's.
4. Mom, for being agreeable when I asked if Raven could live in the basement.
5. My stunning collections of rare Paleolithic fossils, spiderwebs, high-resistance ultrapolymer platings, crash-test dummies from around the world, cat whiskers,

wallpaper, slingshotting rocks, rock posters, ion grids, cottage cheese containers, ouija boards, gold doubloons, iron maidens . . . etc., etc., etc.

6. My beautiful garden of weird weeds, which have clearly missed me and my black thumb.

7. My personal library, which (Great-Aunt Emma would be proud to see) includes <u>Occult Thermodynamics and You</u> AND <u>Secrets of Golem Dominion</u>.

8. All my wondrous and soul-soothing music: Dirge Control, Puppy Glove, Furniture That Sings, Doom Valve, Thee Crypt Divers, Stain Spiral, Split Enzyme, the Larry Beatty Disaster Sequence, Not from Heaven, the Riotous Undead, It Isn't This, Chapter 13 Verse 13, SplatterBoar, etc., etc., etc.

9. My amazing home laboratory and all the experiments I left in it, most of which have been progressing nicely.

10. My pet garbage-eating catfish-goat, who cheerfully recycles all my experiments that haven't progressed so nicely.

11. My ultra-modded Magic 8 Ball, which gives incredibly accurate and insightful answers to all my questions.

12. McFreely's real name, which is Mystery. (Wouldn't you know, her collar was here at home the whole time, in one of Mom's kitchen junk drawers.)

13. And MY name,

Emily!

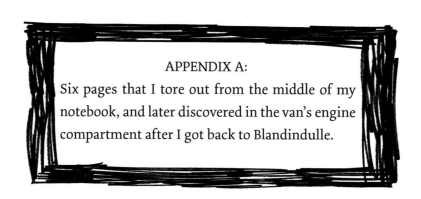

APPENDIX A:

Six pages that I tore out from the middle of my notebook, and later discovered in the van's engine compartment after I got back to Blandindulle.

Day 19

top 13 strangest things in earwig's room:

1. sugarcube diorama of the la brea tar pits
2. mermaid baby in a jar of formaldehyde
3. origami vulture
4. lemur bunker
5. macramé vampire
6. black hole dart gun
7. spiderweb collection
8. rack of custom-built slingshots
9. portable chasm
10. apothecary kit
11. antigravity machine
12. spare forehead

Molly's coffee ring.

molly is stopping at 12. THAT REBEL!!!!

A bit later—alone finally.
Molly is off saying hi to friends.

OK—Molly may be a rebel (a rebel against capitalization if nothing else), but I bet she's won trophies for spelling. I mean—diorama? Apothecary? Impressive.

OK, also,

!!!!!!!!!!!!!!EXCLAMATION POINTS GALORE!!!!!!!!!!!!!!!

Obviously—I have some explaining to do!

Obviously—I have found Molly.

Obviously—I am not Molly.

AND—Molly knows who I really am.

What a day. I found her in the first place I looked. Lucky for me: small town, one overpass.

It's spine-chilling how much Molly and I look alike. No wonder I was fooled by her photos. She is not much <u>like</u> me, though. I've mentioned that she is a popular, well-dressed girl who wins trophies at whatever she does. Also, she smiles a lot. Yeah. Right

Me and Molly.
Guess which one is Molly.

now she's making her extended social rounds of the café. Fine. Gives me some time to write.

Anyway, get this. That girl in Zigzag was right on the money about Molly doing a tour of towns with funny names. She'd been to Boring, Oregon; Skookumchuck, Washington; Pickles Gap, Arkansas; Greasy, Oklahoma; Hippo, Kentucky; and Assinippi, Massachusetts, before hitting Blandindulle. She was at a Laundromat washing the dirty half of her extensive traveling wardrobe (she travels with <u>three</u> suitcases, apparently) when this lady came over and struck up a conversation. Said she had a daughter that looked JUST like Molly. (!) This daughter was away on a cruise to Australia (!!) for a month (!!!). Molly convinced the lady she was on some kind of solo field trip, and the lady invited Molly to crash at her house. Which Molly did.

In MY BEDROOM.

Man oh man oh man oh man oh man.

Anyway, we came here to this café (Blandindulle equivalent of the El Dungeon, I guess) to talk it over. And you know, if it hadn't been for the Sharon and George episode, I probably would have sprinted home without even saying bye to Molly. But if I learned anything from that experience, it's that I probably left home for a reason; going home was not going to cure my amnesia; I probably still had something to learn or do in Blackrock; and if my home was in Blandindulle today, it would most likely still be in Blandindulle next week.

So, if Molly ever makes her way back to our table, maybe I can start getting some useful information out of her. Like for starters, my real name.

Later

I've regained my memories, and what I know makes me want to get amnesia again.

Molly did this to me. I mean the memories, not the amnesia. We were still hanging out at the café in Blandindulle, and she was telling me all this stuff that I of course didn't recall about MY OWN MOTHER, and then boom, she pops out with—OK, I'm not going to even write it down, JUST IN CASE I read this later when I need to keep my amnesia. Anyway, it's like our family swearword, which my mom says all the time. And in my GREAT WISDOM, I'd programmed that word as my failsafe, just in case something awful happened.

Well, something awful HAS happened, and I need to get back to my van and get another dose of amnesia AS SOON AS I CAN!!!!

—Gotta go, Molly is heading this way with a bus ticket for me, more later.

Later

Am back on the bus, headed to Blackrock.

After the joy of regaining my identity came the horror of the dangerous knowledge my mind is so full of. And I am LUCKY that it happened in Blandindulle, and not in Blackrock. Just hope I can get back to the van without encountering Jakey.

Anyway, I made Molly swear that if she encountered me again she would not tell me my name or say my mom's swearword. To give her credit: She felt very bad, and not only paid for my bus ticket back to Blackrock, but promised to come to my aid any time I called. (Let's hope THAT will never happen!)

While waiting for the bus, I got the following information from her:

1. Curls/Ripper sucks his thumb while sleeping. Good Stuff!!
2. She did not tidy my room, under instructions from my mom.
3. She really thinks I need to tidy my room.
4. She thinks I should know that there are several science experiments in my room that are looking VERY unsanitary.
5. She considers me a "creative" type, but she shook her head when she said it.
6. She was amazed to find only identical black sleeveless dresses in my wardrobe.
7. She had a really hard time beating any of the high scores on the video games at my house.
8. She thought all my music was completely unlistenable and does not see how anyone could consider Dirge Control their favorite band.

9. What she loves about new towns is meeting new people. Meeting . . . lots . . . of new . . . people.

10. She and Curls/Ripper did indeed meet some elderly lady in Turniptown, Pennsylvania, who said that Molly reminded her of an old friend in a tiny town called Blackrock.

11. After much argument, Molly finally promised she would NOT show up in Blackrock unless I actually called and asked her to come.

12. Molly misses ~~Bratwurst and Toulouse~~ Tuffy and Tweety a whole heap of a lot. Belgium, those names.

13. My mom never mistook Molly for me. Heartwarming.

OK—Bus is pulling into Blackrock! Time to get down to some serious forgetting!!

APPENDIX B:

Eleven pages that I tore out of the front of my notebook and discovered in the van's wheel-well after I got back to Blandindulle.

Thursday the 12th

Dear Diary,

Welcome to my world, little black book. Don't expect to be addressed as "Dear Diary" anymore. Do expect to have strange liquids spilled on you, and bugs pressed in you, even though I have other books just for strange liquids and pressed bugs, and for gravestone rubbings, bad poetry, good poetry, foreign candy wrappers, cat drawings, cat+monster drawings, robot+cat+monster drawings . . . just to name a few.

The reason I need another black book in my life right now is that I've just gotten the strangest letter from my Great-Aunt Emma, and I have a feeling that diary-worthy adventures are inevitable.

Here's the letter:

Note—I took out
this letter for
strategic purposes
on Tuesday the 17th!

Haven't decided just what to do yet. Still very busy with golem project, which began as a way of making the best of a bad situation. It all started when my cats caught this raven. Cats are vicious, violent, bloodthirsty beast-creatures, you know? Anyway, I stepped in just in time. But too late to save the bird . . . as she was. I happened to be making a golem in my basement that week, and the brain and heart came at the perfect time. This was about a month ago. Right now I'm putting on the final touches before I bring her out of anesthesia. She's going to be my driver. Possibly bodyguard, too. I'll teach her to make sandwiches just how I like them. And maybe a little judo and diamond cutting, if I have time. And now I'm thinking she can help me out in this Blackrock place with this whole inheritance thing.

Friday the 13th

Animated the golem and named her Raven. Man, I did a good job on her. Spent part of the money Great-Aunt Emma sent getting her some nice clothes and a pricy wig. I am never getting pulled over again!

I have a rough plan for this whole inheritance thing now. It goes a little something like this:

1. Develop technology for completely blocking and restoring memory.
2. Create foolproof memory backup device in case of disaster.
3. Install devices into van.

4. Program Raven for the next month.
5. Go to Blackrock.
6. Send Great-Aunt Emma's employee Rachel on a long cruise.
7. Set up Raven and myself in her place.
8. Back up memory.
9. Block out memory.
10. Identify and neutralize the enemy.
11. Take possession of my inheritance.
12. Restore memory.
13. Learn important lesson about ~~life laughter friendship~~ how cool it is to have a golem who follows your every command.

Oh man, I have some lab tinkering to do.

Saturday the 14th

I made the memory backup device. It wasn't that tough. The only tricky part was programming a sorter to organize all my memories into categories as it stored them. But SOOO worth it! Here's a few of my favorites:

Life lessons on danger of colliding subatomic particles at home—17 memories

Sweeping is fun—89 memories

Hilarious antics of cats—23,957 memories

Guts are slippery—45 memories

Slingshot technique—163 memories

People are charming—2 memories

People are better left alone—234,905 memories

Spiders are truly beautiful—54 memories

State capitals—3 memories

Titles of Surrealist paintings—244 memories

New dress—13 memories

My own birth—1 memory

Horrendous nightmare—3,445 memories

Sunday the 15th

Have been experimenting all day with memory-blocking device and, you know, it's really hard to learn from your experiment when the experiment is to block your memory. Had to make myself a sign:

HEY, AMNESIA GIRL!

YOU ARE CONDUCTING AN EXPERIMENT

YOU HAVE JUST BLOCKED OUT YOUR MEMORY

PLEASE POWER UP THE TAPE BACKUP AND ENTER

COMMAND STRING 923RESTORE0815MEM

TO RESTORE YOUR MEMORY

FROM THE LAST SAVED VERSION

OR COMMAND STRING 668CONCATENATE0815MEM

IF YOU WANT TO REMEMBER YOUR AMNESIA, TOO

OR COMMAND STRING &$$INVOKE MYST0815MEM

IF YOU WANT YOUR CAT'S MEMORIES INSTEAD

OR COMMAND STRING 13*13BLACKOUT

FOR ANOTHER ELEVEN MINUTES OF AMNESIA

Monday the 16th

I got the memory-backup and memory-block devices working and installed them under the seats in my van. Did not have time to create independent memory-restore device but I did add a timer function to the memory-block device so I can just specify how long the amnesia lasts. Will start myself out with thirty days. I doubt it will take me that long to get things in Blackrock under control, but just in case.

I got Raven a fake ID and a title to the van in her name. I got the tickets for the cruise for Rachel, and some travel postcards all written up to my mom, for Rachel to mail for me. I got my mom convinced that I won this cruise to Australia and won't be back for a month. GOOD STUFF!

I have so much on my mind with all these preparations that I almost can't wait to lose my memory.

Tuesday the 17th

Spent the day loading the van, convincing my cats they are coming with me, convincing my mom that my "friend" Raven can take the best care of my cats while I'm gone, convincing my mom that my "friend" Raven should drive me to the airport in "her" crazy van, tolerating my mom's tears and hugs, taking mental snapshots of my home, and hoping my memory-block device's timer function works exactly as expected!

Skibbly plagues on my luck today!!!! We broke down about an hour away from Blackrock. No service station in sight, so Raven and I opened the engine compartment, and a blast of fire shot up and got Raven's wig, and I had to pull it off and stamp on it and tear some of the worst burned chunks off. Stupid pricy flammable wig.

Anyway, the engine was a mess, but I couldn't even touch it until it cooled off, so Raven and I took a walk to look for water, since I forgot to pack any in all the confusion. She has an excellent sense of where to dig for water, that Raven. We had to dig for a while using only a spork and a screwdriver, but we eventually hit a gusher, and filled up all our pockets and cheeks and cuppy hands, and ran back to the van, and splashed the engine, and got well steamed. Looks like certain essential engine parts have been ruined in the fire. Man, I wish I had more memories about "storing spare essential engine parts in the van, just in case" and fewer about "telemarketers I have cursed."

Still Tuesday—a lot later

Finally got the van running again, mostly by using strands of Raven's wig to tie together engine parts that looked like they went together. I actually have no idea why we are rolling down the highway at this moment, unless the spirit of Great-Aunt Emma is moving this van. Will definitely pack spare essential engine parts for my next adventure.

Very late Tuesday

Things have gotten super hectic!!!! We finally rolled into Blackrock, and right away got into trouble when Raven nearly drove the van into a cop car that was just sitting in the middle of an intersection with its lights off. Blasted pigfarks! She swerved so hard the passenger door went flying open and I almost shot out of the van—would have, if she hadn't grabbed my arm and yanked

9

me back in! Good old life-saving golem!!!!!! The cop woke up then and started driving after us. And so that's why right now we're involved in a medium-speed car chase through the streets of Blackrock! Not the way I would have chosen to make our entrance into town!! Thank badness I already did all of Raven's programming! Once I get my memory erased, she is going to drop me off somewhere in town and then hide the van. She'll go to the café Great-Aunt Emma told me about and give Rachel her cruise tickets. Oh man I wish I had more time to get ready.

One last Polaroid before things get too crazy:

OK. Camera has just gone smashing to the back of the van. I guess that was my first and last photo of Blackrock. And I just want to take this opportunity to pat myself on the back for creating a nice, stable, competent golem who can calmly steer us through a medium-speed car chase and never bug me about why I am sitting here just writing in my diary.

OK. Am arming myself with slingshot, pen, diary. Will rip out these pages in a moment and hide them in the van. Am wishing myself good luck and happy forgetting! SEE YOU ON THE OTHER SIDE!!!

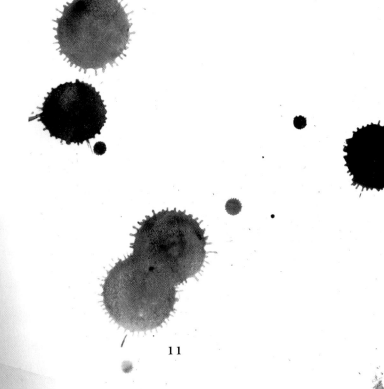

APPENDIX C:

Two letters that came in the mail three months after I got back to Blandindulle.

hey earwig,
what's up,
 so it's been three months! remember?
I DO! also jakey knows I'm not you.
he figured it out a while ago. but
anyway we're in pflugerville,
texas and all the kids thought
I was you! HA! HA! next month
we're stopping to see sharon
and george and get my ponies.
you better have left my bedroom
neat. no, for real.

                    molly

P.S. I totally deserve a trophy
    for being THE BEST crystal
    ball reader ever !!!

Hi Earwig,

Nice trick you played on me! But thats okay. I
knew when you came to see me with your cats you
were lieing. I actually cant hear animals thoughts but
it was a cool plan so I didnt want to spoil it for
you. I mean all that ameshia for nothing. I know you
thouht I would tell Attikol about your black rock. I
was going to since it would be relly nice to go home
again. But then I thouht I could just wait and give
you a chance to help me out. Since you owe me bigtime
after all. Haha well what I mean is: after all YOU
ARE MY FRIEND.

Molly is a good pal so Im not mad but I still miss you.
I hope we can hang out again soon.

Your friend
Jakey

PS my parrot's name is Lily!

Get Lost

It's double the trouble—
watch out for

Emily®
the Strange

Stranger and Stranger

13 cool things you'll find in the next installment of
Emily's diary:

1. OtherMe
2. Epic sewer murals
3. The Manifesto of Strange
4. Cat translator
5. Binary Larry
6. Radiac abrasive lightning rods
7. The Ladies of the Sillifordville Science Club
8. Spy diapers
9. Grand Ravenesque fiascos
10. A sun spigot
11. The family poltergeist
12. Master pranks
13. Venus Fang Fang